The Fox
And The
Raven

DEE CAREY

Writers' Branding
(877) 608-6550
www.writersbranding.com
media@writersbranding.com

Contents

Acknowledgments

I wish to thank my family and my critique partner, Steve Yates. Also, thank you Amelia, who gave my confidence back.

Chapter 1

· · · · · · · · · · ·

I don't know how much longer I can take this. This thing on my leg hurts like I have never been hurt before. Hanging in mid-air is not to my liking. I started to whimper, even though I was certain no one would hear me. Suddenly the sky above me cast a shadow that grew ever darker, an ominous portent to my current predicament.

It was a big black bird, very big and very black. I hid my face hoping it wouldn't harm me further. It landed right beside me. "Well, little fellow, how did you get yourself into this fix?" it asked. Apparently, it had no desire to devour me.

"I'dunno. I was walking alone without a care and suddenly, I was confined in this contraption. It grabbed over my paw and I can't get out of it." The bird's shiny black beak clicked as I spoke. There was not a bit of color on him. His eyes, even his feet, were as black as his feathers. Usually things that are black are dark in demeanor as well. I grew cautious, but this very large bird seemed to understand my situation and appeared ready to assist me in getting free.

I was trapped in a thicket, with all sorts of bushes and brambles about. The ground was soft and yielded to my weight even though I am no larger than the cat that chased me from the stables. Most foxes are far larger than I, but when I was forced into this form, my torturer wanted to make certain that I would not survive as I am nearly too small to hunt. However, I am also cunning and quickly learned to fend for myself. I made a near fatal error when I ventured into this thicket. The earth is soft, and I fear, had I gone further, I would have gone into a bed of quicksand. It was an area I'd never hunted before and the mouse I chased across the meadow ran into the thick brush. The raven cocked its head to the side and seemed to assess my situation. It ruffled its feathers then combed them back into shape.

"Can you help me, friend raven?"

"I can," it said, and flew off.

Maybe I should have asked if it would help me. It flew directly above me carrying a stone in its beak. Far above me, the bird began to dive then released the stone, which hit the cord and released me. I was free. Free, but with no feeling in my paw. I stamped it against the ground. Nothing. I did it several more times and found some relief. The raven landed beside me as I thumped the earth.

"Why are you doing that?"

"It stops the hurting for a time." Then I bent over and licked the offending paw. But it still had the sensation of not being connected to the rest of me.

"Do you know why this happened to me? I never hurt anyone except for food."

"Nor have I, friend. I know of no reason you would be so harmed. However, my master most assuredly will be able to fix you."

"Your master?"

"He's not truly my master, as I come and go as I please."

"Are you his pet?" The raven did not like my last question as indicated by ruffled feathers.

"I am a lady, and you will not speak to me in that fashion. I am no man's pet. Suffice it to say he's a friend of mine." She turned her back on me and strode out to the meadow. After a few moments, she turned and asked, "Well, are you coming?"

As no other option presented itself, I limped along behind her. My paw stung each time I touched the ground.

"Wait up," I called. The bird stopped and turned.

"What's wrong?" she asked.

"What's wrong? Well, let's see. I'm too small, my paw hurts and I don't even know who I am following. Who are you?"

"I'm called Fechin. It means little raven."

"Why would someone name you little?"

The raven snickered and continued on her intended path. She'd only walked a short distance before she turned back and asked, "What's your name, friend fox?"

I limped forward and sat back on my haunches. "I'll tell you if you will slow down, please. You are far larger than I, your stride is longer, and I find it hard to keep up. Though I do appreciate you're not flying."

"I understand. I will walk slower. But my question is, what are you called?"

Just then, my paw stung as if attacked by a horde of bees. I shook it violently to ease the sensation. The action somewhat diminished the pain, yet I feared it would not support my body. I gently put weight on it and though it was not comfortable, I found it bearable.

"I'm Flynn."

We continued in silence for some time until I espied a castle in the distance. I'd never beheld such an imposing structure. It gleamed pink in the sunrise with sparkling glints over the surface of the stone. The towers rose above the castle like hands raised in prayer. As we passed through the portcullis, I was in awe. The grounds were covered with flowers of every color and kind. Everywhere I looked, someone was happily engaged in some sort of task.

Suddenly Fechin took flight. I grew frightened. I was so small I feared I could not defend myself should the need arise. Why would she leave me like this? She knew I was unprotected. Within moments, she returned with a tiny mouse in her feet. She pushed it toward me and bid me eat. I was very hungry and consumed the creature instantly. Fechin ruffled her feathers then groomed them back in place saying, "Come with me."

She did not allow me time to cleanse myself as I did after meal, no matter how meager. I hesitated and she pushed me with her large head, toward the majestic palace. I thought we would go through the main door, but I was wrong. She was leading me to a side entrance that was covered with vines and moss, apparently to hide its existence. I was totally unable to discern the opening, until Fechin pecked at a particular rock. It opened like the maw of a massive sea creature. We entered and at once we were going down a series of stairs. There were steps for a time, then a flat landing. I was grateful for the flat landing from time to time, as I was nearly out of breath. It seemed we were traveling to the very center of the earth, so long did we descend.

~ ~ ~

MERLIN

Where is that damned bird? When I don't want her around, she's underfoot and when I do I can't find her. The thought no more than passed through my consciousness when I heard the flapping of her overlarge wings. She was home. I prayed she found something that would lead us to finding the culprit responsible for Arthur's illness. I knew it was no common malady.

In the past month, he'd gone from a strong, vibrant regent, to the mere shell of a man. I turned, to ask her what she learned, only to find her gone once again. She irked me to no end. In the heat of my anger, I opened my mouth to yell at her when I saw her standing in the stairwell with a tiny fox beside her.

"Now what fool stray did you bring me?"

The bird replied in the voice of a haughty queen, as she felt she was, since she ruled the rookery. "He is not a fool. That was most unkind of you. Though he is slightly injured I'm certain he can be of assistance to us."

"Injured how? He looks fine to me."

The raven nodded, saying, "He was caught in a snare. The loop seems to have affected his paw. He says he has no feeling in it."

I turned to the little creature and it blinked with a look of a startled fawn. His gaze made me want to care for him.

"All right, enough with the sad eyes. You may stay and I'll see what I can do for your injury."

The skin didn't appear to be a problem, but it hung at an odd angle when he lifted it from the ground.

"Fechin, what's his name?" I asked.

The little fox blinked and said, "I'm Flynn."

"Oh, Irish fellow, are you?"

His fur raised along a ridge on his back. "Yes, and I'm very proud to be." I smiled and replied, "And well you should be. Irish is a fine thing to be."

The fox blinked, and I noted his foot began to spasm. I took his paw in my palm. It palsied so my entire arm shook. I feared it was beyond my skills.

"Does it hurt, Flynn?"

"Not hurt or pain, it just feels like it isn't attached to me. I'll get used to the sensation, it is not a matter of great concern."

He's one plucky fox, I'll give him that. Maybe he could help us find who is endangering the King.

"Fechin, did you learn anything before you came upon Flynn?" My raven blinked at the fox. Was this some form of communication between the two?

~ ~ ~

MORGAINE

I looked up as someone entered my quarters. Though I was not a favorite of the Queen, her husband, my brother, saw fit I be provided with the proper setting. The room was quite opulent. Velvet drapes and embroidered pillows atop the chairs. The hearth was warm and inviting.

I turned and saw my grampa. "Ah, to whom do I owe the favor of your presence?"

The old but still virile man stood before me. His demeanor was not his usual, one of wisdom, and the man was clearly confused.

"Merlin," I asked, "What is troubling you? I've never seen you look so befuddled."

He smiled and tugged on his full white beard. I remember laying my head against that soft cloud. Those were the times of my greatest joy. We were very close. He taught me all I know, from reading to his special skills. We share a unique bond. I love him still.

"Merlin, please speak to me. Tell me what's got you so out of sorts?" I asked, as I set aside the book of poetry I'd been reading.

"Oh, my precious one, I did not come here to burden you with my problems, but simply to find joy in your company."

I led him to his favorite chair. Though I am a grown woman, still sometimes I yearn to sit and rock with my grampa, as I did when I had troubles as a child. Thus I kept his favorite seat, in my home.

I had no blood grandparents, so the wizard was my grampa. It was the one relationship in my life that I cherished.

I'd long ago made peace with my brother. Mordred, my son, however, harbors an unbelievable bitterness. Arthur has recognized him as the heir, unless he and Guinevere have a child. I know Arthur will provide for our son.

"Merlin, you have yet to tell me the reason for your sour disposition."

"Come now, child, I'm not sour. I'm just concerned about Arthur."

"I've just come from Avalon, so I don't know what you're alluding to. Is he ill or injured? I know he still trains, though he no longer enters the jousts."

"Well, my dear he is ill, very ill. And he grows weaker by the day."

I felt his concern. He cared as much for Arthur as he did me.

"Grampa, surely you can do something for him?"

He shook his head, saying, "That's part of the reason I'm here. Nothing I've done has eased him. I hoped you might assist me with your vast knowledge of healing herbs. Will you help?"

"Of a certainty, I will do all in my power to heal my brother."

I put my arm through his and we walked to the King's suite. Merlin tapped on the door and Guinevere opened it. She embraced the wizard and glared at me. While Arthur and I were reconciled, Her Highness was as opposed to me as she always was. Little Bitch.

Walking to my brother's bedside, I took his hand in mine. He was so fevered, I felt as if his touch scorched me.

"Merlin, we have to cool him at once. His fever must be broken."

"I know, Morgaine, but how? We can't move him to the lake. He's too weak to move."

"Then we must bring the water to him. Have a tub brought here and fill it with the coldest spring water in Camelot."

The wizard looked at me as if I had two heads.

"Hurry, we've little time to waste," I said, urging him into action. He left the room faster than I have ever seen the old man move. Guinevere pulled my arm, removing my hand from Arthur's forehead.

"You leave him alone, you witch. I'll not have your fool spells and rituals kill the King."

"So, even though I have the skills to save him, you would let him die, because you hate me?"

A look of abject fear swept over her features.

"Yes, no," she whined, "I don't know." She rushed to the door and ran down the corridor screaming, "Merlin, Merlin, help me. I'm so frightened and confused."

Little Twit.

~ ~ ~

ELAINE

I saw her running down the hallway yelling like a banshee. The woman possesses no queenly virtues. She's not fit to rule. Nor do I have any wish to reign. But I would have what she's stolen from me. She has the love of a king, a palace, the finest clothes and even her own pure-bred, snow-white mare. Why, why then does she have, even the love of the one man I have ever desired?

She left the door open when she fled. Merlin and Morgaine were too involved with Arthur to notice me. I snuck in and hid within the folds of a massive tapestry hanging opposite Arthur's bed. I knew I would be undetected, as here is where I've hidden many times as I watched my love in slumber.

I've also entered his quarters as a lady-in-waiting to the Queen. She likes to share her meal with Arthur since he is too weak to join her in the hall. Daily I bring a meal made especially for her.

~ ~ ~

MERLIN

Ah, little heartbroken Elaine. Do you think I cannot see you? Your hatred of the Queen has blinded you to other issues. I had to know more of her reasons for hiding in the King's quarters. Could she be a spy, and if so for whom? I turned back to see Arthur, a pale, frail husk of a man. At least his senses were intact.

"Merlin," he said, near to gasping for breath, "Can you identify what has befallen me? It is something you have seen before?"

It was a telling question. One I dared not answer. True, it appeared to be a malady I'd encountered before, yet those I saw did not survive. This I could not reveal to the King. Hope was the only thing keeping him alive. I would not take that from him.

Morgaine still held his hand, as his eyes begged me for answers. She brushed his unruly hair back off his forehead, all the while assessing his body temperature.

A knock sounded at the door. I opened it and many servants entered. Three men carrying a tub and five more baring buckets of cool, spring water. I directed them where to place the tub. Once the tub was filled, I thanked and dismissed them.

"Morgaine, help me undress Arthur and get him in the tub."

"Merlin!" she said, aghast.

"I'm his sister, not his wife."

"I recall the relationship did not trouble you on another occasion."

"I know, I know, but things are different now."

~ ~ ~

FECHIN (raven)

Merlin is not the only one who senses the presence of one unseen. Yet neither he nor Morgaine pay heed. So busy are they, with their own concerns, they pay me no mind.

As Merlin and Morgaine are tending Arthur they did not notice as I flew out the window. Elaine also chose to leave unnoticed, however so intent on leaving unseen by the people in the room neither did she note my departure.

I waited in the thickly foliated tree near the postern gate. Finally, Elaine emerged, looking furtively in every direction. Apparently satisfied, she had escaped unobserved, she lifted her skirts and ran pell-mell to the nearby wood.

Few lived in the wood as Arthur had provided well for all his subjects. So, I wondered who she was meeting and for what purpose? The only person that I knew who ever lived there was an old crotchety woman, folks believed to be a witch. Over the years I'd watched her, she never engaged in what one would call witchcraft. The old woman was probably dead by now as many years had passed since I last saw her. She lived just inside the wood and her home was well concealed. Few even knew of her existence. I discovered her years ago on an evening when Merlin and I had exchanged heated words and I flew off in a rage.

So, what did Elaine want with Haga? Elaine was a tall woman, so she had to duck her head in order to enter Haga's home. I heard her cackle as she drew Elaine by her elbow through the door.

"Old woman, you have no reason to be so rough," she said, as she shrugged free of the woman's grasp.

Not wanting to miss a word of this clandestine conversation, I flew up onto the roof and burrowed my way through the thatch, just enough to observe and hear, yet not be discovered.

"Well, little missy, what is it you now wish to procure?" The hag again grasped Elaine, holding her wrist tightly within her gnarled fingers.

The girl appeared frightened as she tried to remove the vise grip from her wrist. She started to whimper and Haga released her, roughly throwing her against a table strewn with jars and tiny wooden chests.

"Now look what you've done. Get down and retrieve every, powder, potion, and herb or I'll snatch you bald."

"Yeees, Ma'am." The girl lost her haughty demeanor and fell to her knees to do as she was bid.

I felt it was not a harsh enough punishment. Certain Merlin would mete out a greater retribution, I eased my way out of the thatch, carefully as I wanted the women unaware of my presence. Once free of the roof's covering, I flew to a nearby pine tree. I wanted to know the true reason behind Elaine's visit to Haga. My wait paid off as I watched the girl emerge. I cocked my head as I listened to the old woman's direction.

"Remember, lass, one will heal and two will kill, so proceed with the greatest caution."

~ ~ ~

FLYNN

Morgaine had thoughtfully covered me with a blanket as I slept in Merlin's quarters. He'd done all he could to mend my paw, the throbbing and stinging was gone but it still troubled me if I put my full weight on it.

Though well rested, I was alone. Merlin and Morgaine had not yet returned. Tending the ailing king, no doubt.

Looking out the window, I noted the sun was near to setting, I'd slept longer than I thought. Perhaps, the rest had aided me.

Jumping from the bed on three legs, I began to explore the realm of the great wizard Merlin. His quarters were quite orderly, not what I expected from one who dabbled in sorcery. There are more things in his dwelling that I could ever have imagined. This place is amazing I've never seen anything like it. Shelves and shelves of books, far greater than the number I believed existed.

Then I caught the scent of a mouse. It was familiar, but different from my usual fare.

I could hear him rummaging through a pile of parchment on the wizard's desk. I jumped up onto the massive furniture sending a large book and many vials smashing to the floor with a resounding crash. The sound did not deter me, nor did the pain in my paw. I was after the mouse.

Between two books on a shelf was a small space. There, the mouse stood. At least I thought it was a mouse. It was the same size except for its ears. They were very large and its coat was a soft brown, not the grey of field mice. Boldly it walked from between the volumes and smiled. Smiled? Then it sprinted along the edge of the shelf. I followed on the floor, heedless of the damage I was causing. I knocked over books, strewn papers, set an inkwell on its side, and scattered whatever else was in my path. Suddenly, the door to the workroom burst open and an enraged Merlin stomped in.

"You fool fox, what is the meaning of this destruction?"

I froze, as I had no reasonable explanation. Just then, Morgaine grabbed the wizard's arm.

"Please, Merlin, I'm certain he meant no harm."

"No harm? How does the creature expect to right this situation?"

At that moment, Fechin flew in and landed beside the brown mouse with the large ears, upon a high shelf.

"You all right, Allowishes?" She knows him by name? How can this be?

"Fechin," I called.

"Who is this small one you address as Allowishes?"

All the while I was doing my best to elude Merlin, who was chasing me with a vengeance. Fechin flew to the sorcerer's shoulder and spoke softly in his ear. I could not hear what he said, but it had an impact on Merlin. At once his countenance softened. The raven flew the short distance across the room and set down on the floor beside me.

"Don't worry, Flynn. You shan't be punished. That is unless you intended to cause this mess?"

"No, I never wanted to damage anything. I was just hungry. I've not eaten since you freed me."

"No wonder you're hungry. That was two days ago." With that pronouncement, the mouse slipped back between the books.

"Don't worry Allowishes, he won't eat you. Flynn, he's a friend, a friend with magical properties."

~ ~ ~

ALLOWISHES

Whew, I wish one of my magical properties was to be unseen. I'm not sure if I can trust this fox. Fechin, seeing my distrust, began to laugh.

"Allowishes, don't worry. Flynn is a good fox. Besides, if he annoys you, you do have the option to be a bear."

"Yes," I replied, "But he doesn't know that."

Again, the raven laughed. "I'd wager he would figure it out right quick."

Flynn nodded, saying, "Yes, I would reason that out in a hurry. You wouldn't have to show me twice."

I stepped out into plain view.

"Do we have an understanding then?"

"We do," he replied.

"That's just fine," Merlin interjected.

"Who is going to clean my workroom?"

"I will great wizard, 'twas my fault after all," Flynn said.

"No so friend mouse, it was my doing. I'll help you."

Closing my eyes, I reversed time to the point before the chaos ensued. Within moments, order was restored. When I opened my eyes, the fox stood gaping. He was beyond astounded.

"How," he said, "Did you do that?"

Fechin laughed and said, "I told you, magical properties." Flynn closed his mouth and shook his head.

"That's the most amazing thing I've ever seen."

"Stick around, Flynn, there is much more to see," I replied, confident we would be fast friends.

Chapter 2

. . . .

ELAINE

Why? Why doesn't he get better? I've done exactly as Haga said. My heart is torn asunder. She thrives and he is near death. I must see him.

I stole along the corridor leading to his room, careful to remain unseen. As Guinevere is visiting her father it would not bode well for me, if I were discovered in the king's suite without Her Majesty present. I shall be very careful, but I must see him. After silently closing the large oak door, I heard footsteps in the hallway. Quickly I went to my usual hiding place, the wall tapestry. The door was slowly opened, and a gentle knock sounded, awaking my love.

"Enter," he called, and Morgaine came into the room.

"How are you today, Brother?"

"I'm not in pain, but I grow weaker by the hour. How I wish I could have my vigor restored."

"As do I, Arthur. What measures have been taken to restore you to good health?"

"Each day Elaine brings me a tonic she gets from the old healer, Haga. But it does nothing, save to sicken me further."

I know this to be true, but the reason escapes me. I have always been careful to give him the proper container just as the healer directs.

"Does Elaine bring anything else besides the potion?"

"No, just the potion. When Gwen is here she brings a tonic for her."

"But no food? No other drink?"

Arthur heaved a sigh, and I was astounded at the effort it required. He is right. He grows weaker with each passing day. I must help him. He is so very tired from Morgaine's brief visit, I'm certain she will leave soon. I will then hasten to the healer. Surely she will know what is happening to him.

Morgaine leaned over her brother then kissed his forehead as he slept and drew the blanket up over his shoulders. I waited until I heard her footsteps diminish as she went down the hallway.

Certain no one would see me as I left the king's quarters, I emerged from behind the tapestry and exited as quickly as possible. I fled the castle by the postern gate as it was unlikely I would there encounter anyone of note. My heart in my throat, I ran across the meadow into the thicket wherein Haga dwelt.

The small wood was dense and dark. I could barely see the well-worn path to her door. The trees and brambles were closing around me. The usual woodland sounds, the birds twittering, mice scampering through the leaves—all were silent. Running blindly, I hoped I was going to her hut and not getting irrevocably lost. If I became lost, not a soul would miss me, nor would anyone search for me. My heart pounded so loud, I feared whatever is out there could hear. Everywhere I looked, the moonlight cast frightening shadows. I started to run, through the brambles that tore at my clothing.

It was taking far too long to reach Haga's cottage and now there was no light at all. It was night and I was scared and alone. Who knew what creatures came out into the darkness? Certain I would become a meal for a wolf or a bear, I sat down and cried.

I felt I was being watched but saw not a soul. It was too dark to see more than a few feet. Whatever it was, I prayed it was not hungry. Overwrought with tears and fears, I finally gave into slumber.

~ ~ ~

FLYNN

Though I was not certain the girl was an innocent, nevertheless I felt pity for her. She had no family and I'd never seen her in the company of another lass. Perhaps she was friendless as well.

My stomach growled, and I resumed my hunt. Mice and moles were plentiful in the thicket and I had missed my evening repast. I'd come to enjoy sharing a meal with Fechin and Merlin. We exchanged the happenings of our days and provided what information we could. As I was new to palace life, each tale was a revelation to me. More importantly we reported what, if anything, we learned that might point to the cause of Arthur's illness. The poor man was certainly no longer the Arthur of Camelot the minstrels sang of.

With little difficulty I secured a mouse. I was careful to examine it closely as I had no desire to consume Allowishes. Though he was a rodent, he seemed to me to be so much more than the usual mice of the fields.

I laid down near to the girl, keeping a close eye on her. Once the dawn broke, she should be able to find her way back to the castle.

She awakened and searched frantically, looking about her in every direction. It was clear she was still unaware of her location. She began to cry again. I hate human tears. There seems to be little reason for them, save to gain sympathy. I pondered how I could lead her back without her hearing me speak. It is only recently I learned some humans could hear and understand animals. But to speak to her would break my confidence with Fechin and Merlin.

While she still sobbed, I edged closer and closer. She hiccupped and blew her nose on the scrap of linen she drew from her pocket. Then she dried her tears and looked at me.

"Well, little fox, do you know where we are?"

I nodded and took the corner of her apron in my teeth and tugged on it. She stood and took several hesitant steps toward me. I continued to pull at her apron, so she tried to take it from my grasp then resumed her crying. Releasing the cloth, I sat back on my haunches beside her. We sat there for quite some time until she started to talk to herself.

"He's not dangerous. Maybe he does know how to get out of here. I'll let him lead me. At this point I've nothing to lose."

I again took the corner of her apron in my teeth. As I tugged at it gently, she began to follow me. She acted as if each step was into greater danger. I'd never encountered a more timid soul.

We walked silently for hours, the lass still sniffling. The poor child was so fearful and hopeless, I feared for her. If she didn't develop a stronger countenance, she might not make it in this troubled world. As the sun stood high and its shine illuminated the meadow, she began to recognize her surroundings. Once I was certain she knew where the castle was, I dropped the corner of her apron and slipped quietly back into the wood.

The small mouse I'd consumed was not enough sustenance for an entire day, so I headed back to the castle and whatever amazing meal Merlin had secured for us. I was astounded how quickly I desired the fare of the humans over my own hunting. My mouth watered just contemplating what a tempting plate would be put before me.

I prayed I would not encounter the lady I aided as she might try to speak to me. Not that I feared her, but the fewer persons who knew I could talk, the better. It is easy to be overlooked if the one observing believes any information heard could not be repeated.

~ ~ ~

MORGAINE

I find it rather amusing that Merlin believes his critters think he is the one who cooks their meals. I have no problem with it, but someday the truth will out. To my mind at least, Fechin, is aware who the chef is. The fox cares little if he is fed, so probably does not give much thought to the matter. I've prepared a good-sized goose, which should satisfy the group. After I cleaned the area of cooking utensils, I called to Merlin.

"Merlin, it is safe to call your friends. The meal is presented as if by magic."

The old sorcerer smiled, a twinkle in his eye, and gave me a soft kiss.

"Thank you, my child. I appreciate your keeping my little charade a secret."

"I don't mind, Merlin, but it seems a little silly. You are the greatest mage of all time. Why does it matter or not if others think you can cook as well?"

"Morgaine, I wish I could explain it, but the reasons are a mystery to me as well. Someday I may learn why, but for now I truly appreciate your aid in this silly secret."

I wondered if I should relate what I learned in the store room, or should I keep it as my secret? The tallies do not add up. There are far fewer goods than show on the counting sheets. Perhaps I will wait until Arthur is well. No use worrying him further, it would only stall his recovery.

Apparently, someone had rung a dinner bell. They all piled in as if they were bees escaping a burning hive. Even little Allowishes came running from his hiding place between the books. I'd set out the plates each a size to accommodate the diner. Even though Flynn was a newcomer he quickly found his proper seat.

The head of the most hungry rose first. As tiny as he was, he had a most voracious appetite. In his tiny voice he squeaked, "May I have some of that wonderful-smelling stew."

"Of course, Allowishes, there is plenty for all, you need not rush," I said, as I filled the smallest bowl and placed it in front of the wee mouse. Once all were seated, Merlin bowed his head and asked a blessing from the sky, the trees, and all of nature. Each consumed his meal in his own fashion.

"Lady Morgaine," the fox said, addressing me.

"I thank you for this wonderful stew, it was truly the most wonderful thing I have ever eaten."

I smiled inwardly, as Merlin loudly cleared his throat.

"Flynn, I have prepared this repast, not the Lady Morgaine. She, too, is my guest."

The poor fox looked forlorn. "I am so sorry, my Lord Merlin. As Morgaine was out of our sight for such a long time and you were gone only moments, I assumed 'twas she who prepared the meal."

The wizard harrumphed, saying, "Well, she didn't. I did, with magic."

~ ~ ~

HAGA

These imbeciles, how simple are they? Thinking putting me out of their sight will keep me from my revenge. They shall learn in due time what it truly means to cross a green witch. Fortunately, few know of the extent of my skills. I am, however, known as a healer of some repute, thus I have their respect and there will come a time when I shall have their fear as well. Even the tremors of that foolish sorcerer, will warm the cockles of my heart.

It is a shame they allow their emotions and desires for immediate gratification, cripple them. Time is my friend. I do not venture where those fools flock.

The one who is most deserving of my wrath is that simpering bitch Guinevere. She shall come to realize her beauty is not coin.

Hearing the rap of knuckles against my door, I called out, "Who's there?"

"Mistress Haga, tis I, Sir Lancelot."

At a loss for the reason a knight would seek me out, I was hesitant. Usually when a knight, or any man for that matter, was sick or injured, I was summoned to them. They did not come to my door themselves, an emissary was always sent.

"Are you injured?"

"No, I seek your aid on another matter."

"And what matter would that be?" I've learned the greater your knowledge of those who come to you, the less difficult it is to discern their true motives.

"Mistress, I intend you no harm. I simply have need of your skills. Please admit me."

Slowly and timidly I allowed him entrance. I have naught to fear, however I wish for him to believe, I am but an old frightened, helpless woman.

Using the most fearful voice possible I said, "How can I aid you?" I'd not seen this man before and wondered how he learned of my powers.

As soon as I spoke, he fell to his knees, with his hands raised in supplication. It was clear to me he wanted no one to know his reason for being here.

"Please, my Lady Haga, you must help me. My heart is rent in two. I care deeply for the woman but also feel compelled to serve the King."

My lady, I like the sound of that. Soon, Elaine, soon. Be patient. Ever progressing at a steady pace, will get you your reward. No one will impede you if they do not perceive you are running.

"And what is it you would have me do Sir Knight?"

"Mistress Haga, I would have you make for me a potion that will make me irresistible to the Lady who sat beside the king at the jousts last spring. I want her to yearn to be with me."

"You ask a lot. And how will I benefit? Everything has its price, lad."

The so-called brave knight is both frightened and hopeful. Word of my powers has spread.

"Ask of me whatever you wish. I am yours to command." Just what I love, a malleable minion.

"In due time, you puny excuse for a man, you will receive what you desire, and I will tell you your task. Now go and return after three turnings of the moon."

~ ~ ~

GUINEVERE

I don't how long I've been running. Nothing seems familiar. I'm lost, I really am a twit as I overheard the servants call me.

No one will miss me. Even Arthur won't notice. He's too sick to care. And I have no longing for him. He's old. He must be forty.

Isn't there somewhere out there, a real knight in shining armor? A man with strong arms to hold me and a heart to embrace me. I would be his and he would be mine. Where might my hero be?

I looked up at the hill in this strange meadow, and there on the crest of the knoll, stood a magnificent white steed and upon his back hooves was my knight. His armor glistened in the sun. It was as if a page had been ripped from my diary. All I wished for. It was what I dreamed of and he was coming down the hill for me.

The white horse stopped mere inches from me. As the rider lifted the visor on his helmet, I beheld the deepest blue eyes staring at me. It was as if he were compelled to gaze upon me for his very breath. The compulsion was not his alone, I, too, was so affected.

The knight's face turned red and his tongue seemed to wrap itself into a ball. This pleases me. I like a man rendered speechless by my presence alone. I fixed my gaze upon him until he regained his power of speech.

"My lady, I've admired you from afar and it gives me great pleasure to make your acquaintance."

"My good knight, the pleasure is mine as well. May I ask where you did you see me from afar?"

"I was a latecomer to Arthur's first tournament last spring. I saw you sitting beside the King. Is he a relative?"

Oh, how I wished he was any relative, other than a husband.

"The king is my husband."

I could almost see the knight's heart skip a beat. It was clear he felt the same as I.

He looked away then dropped to one knee, saying, "Please forgive my boldness, Your Highness. I am but your humble servant. My lady how are you called?" he asked in dulcet tones. His voice so soft and deep it tickled my ears.

"I'm Guinevere, Sir…?"

"Lancelot," he replied.

Chapter 3

· · · · · · · · · · ·

FECHIN

"Oh, this does not bode well. All the King needs, on top of illness, countless raids, now he has a faithless wife?"

I watched the pair from my perch in plain view over their heads, but as birds are frequently in trees, they paid me little notice.

This appeared to be their first meeting, but the attraction is palpable. I'd seen the knight on only one occasion, but there was no mistaking his intentions. I prayed their reason and loyalty to the king would halt their ardor. This information must be brought to Merlin's attention. As I took flight, I noted Flynn appeared to be watching the couple as well… He was as still as a cat waiting to pounce. Only his snout protruded the thick grasses. I swooped down beside him, chasing away his prey.

"Sorry, Flynn, but Merlin's fare is far tastier. Come with me. I've something to share with the wizard."

"Oh, is that so? I need to fend for myself if something happens to the Merlin. He'd quite old, you know."

"Yes, he's older than time itself. Have no fears. He's always here, even if he's not. We have to get out of this meadow without them seeing us."

"Them? Who them? I don't see anyone." It was clear the fox was more intent on his lost rodent than on the human couple in field.

The pair continued to gaze, as if moonstruck, into one another's eyes. He embraced her, then quickly dropped his arms.

"You are not mine to hold, but I shall always be at your side when I am needed. For now we must serve Arthur, not besmirch his name."

The fox followed my sight line to the large oak.

"Over there, under the tree I just came from. It's the Queen and a knight I've only seen once before. They appear to be quite fond of each other. The Merlin must needs to know this, but I fear he will not tell the king."

"Why not? If I had a mate I would want to know if she were unfaithful."

"Most would Flynn, but as sick as Arthur is, I am certain Merlin will wish to handle this matter without troubling the King. Come on, I've seen more than I ever wished to gaze upon."

The fox looked up at me, consternation clear upon his features.

"Too true, my friend, I would never have conceived a woman so graced with such riches would betray the man who bestowed them upon her."

As I'd only known the fox a short time I was unsure of his beliefs. I was pleased his feelings mirrored my own.

"We will report what we have seen and trust the Merlin will have a solution for the problem." We continued walking briskly in total silence.

~ ~ ~

MORGAINE

What has caused this normally riotous gathering to become silent? The usual bantering and laughter have taken leave of this group. Merlin was particularly morose.

As I rose to clear the table the wizard waved his hand at Allowishes and at once the table was as before the meal. The old man gave a slight smile to the mouse then loudly cleared his throat.

"Ladies and gentlemen, we have a serious problem. It could destroy not only the king, but the kingdom as well."

The smallest of the group scurried across the table and laid his head against the wizard's hand.

"I know, my little friend, you can only reverse things, not people, but Allowishes, I thank you for your support."

The poor little mouse returned to his niche between the books, clearly dejected.

"What Fechin and Flynn have reported troubles me greatly."

I started for the door, as I thought I could offer no assistance.

"Morgaine, come back, we have need of you as much as the rest." I turned, smoothed my gown, and sat with the others. Grandpa reached for my hand and held it tightly as if it contained a solution. Alas it did not.

A strange noise alerted us that we had an intruder.

"You all stay here. I will handle this small matter while you ponder the more pressing issue." Getting up from the table, I patted the old man's hand and moved in the direction I believed the sound came from.

Standing outside of Merlin's workroom, I heard the shuffling of parchment and a slight clinking noise. Someone was going through the sorcerer's tools and writings. Why? His possessions would not be of use to anyone other than Merlin. Was this then the prank of the youths in the village? I thought not. The children both loved and revered the King's mage. Who then? And why?

I slipped quietly into the room and there I beheld the Lady Elaine. She sat at the large worktable, her head in her hands, sobbing.

I approached her and gently placed my hand on her shoulder. She looked up, raising her tear-stained face and hiccupped.

"Elaine, my child, why are you here in Merlin's quarters? You know it is forbidden unless Merlin bids you enter."

"I know," she whimpered.

"I came to ask for his help, but I couldn't find him, so I decided I would search for a potion to make Arthur love me."

"Elaine, Merlin is not a kitchen witch who whips up a special elixir to make a beloved desire you."

"I understand, but I'm desperate. Arthur must love me, so I can rid him of the treacherous Guinevere."

"The Queen treacherous? I believe you're mistaken Elaine." I did not want the lass to know I, too, was worried by the Queen's behavior, though I knew, Elaine only cared about her love.

She stopped long enough to catch her breath, then began to sob anew.

I took her in my arms, saying, "Hush, Elaine, you must calm yourself. If you keep crying you will make yourself ill."

"Oh, Morgaine, what am I going to do? I simply cannot live without him."

Of course, you can, you silly child.

"I understand, Elaine, right now you must rest. I'll make some tea, then you take a nap. When you wake I'll aid you." She followed me to my quarters.

"You will?" She looked at me skeptically as I prepared her tea.

I replied, "I will." This apparently eased her mind as she took the cup from me and drained it.

Her eyelids grew heavy and she surrendered to sleep.

I knew I should report back to the others, but a strange feeling overtook me. All around me, I felt a barrier that enveloped Elaine as well.

I sat by her as she lay on my bed. She began to snore and turn fitfully.

Finally she settled, and I dozed. Suddenly, she sat up and started speaking.

"We can't, we can't, it's wrong. Lancelot, isn't there another way?"

This revelation paints another section of this convoluted mural. It was clear to me Elaine and Lancelot were in league with one another in some nefarious scheme. Could they somehow have something to do with Arthur's illness? What would they have to gain?

Chapter 4

· · · · · · · · · · · ·

ALLOWISHES

There is something very wrong in Arthur's perfect Camelot. The rest of our little group seems intent on finding the culprit. I, however, reason if we find out the why, the who will present itself. How is this heinous act being carried out?

As I returned to my niche, I pulled out a small piece of parchment and a small black feather. The page I pilfered from Merlin and the feather from Fechin as she slept. Ink was always available as the wizard was constantly writing.

I had to examine every angle, both what I know to be true, what I perceive is false, and most importantly what I need to know.

Deeply immersed in my work I did not notice Fechin and Flynn entered the work room. Alerted by Flynn's sharp yip, I turned and beheld the pair, who seemed out of breath.

"Have you two been running? Or are you just hungry for another of Merlin's magic meals?"

They answered as if with a single voice, "Yes." This pair is very confusing.

"Yes, to which one?"

Fechin ruffled her feathers saying, "We were running to report to Merlin what we have learned, and we are hungry."

Morgaine entered, inquiring, "Where's Merlin?"

I placed my paw on the parchment to mark my place.

"I've not seen him all day."

"I was with him a short while ago, before I found a sobbing Elaine, searching for something to make the king set aside the queen."

"Foolish girl," I said. Flynn interjected before I was able to say more.

"I wonder how she got here before us. Is she still here?"

"Yes," Morgaine reported. "I've given her a sleeping potion and put her in my quarters to rest."

Was this wise? I thought. "Morgaine, is she unguarded?"

"Why would she need to be confined?"

Still holding my paw on the parchment, I said, "If she was snooping, why was she doing so? Such a matter would cause me to be wary and give reason to secure her until the Wizard returns."

Morgaine was quiet, apparently considering the issue.

"Quite right, Allowishes. Flynn, go and stay outside of my rooms until Merlin returns."

The little fox flicked his tail and set out to do her bidding.

"You are not truly fearful of Elaine?" I asked.

"Nay, not of the girl herself, but of whoever is using the simple lass."

"Ah, yes. I too am wary of such a situation. She is as malleable as clay, and not the sharpest nib in the quill box." Morgaine came to the table-like structure I've improvised to write upon. She gently, but very firmly, took the scrap I'd been writing on.

"And what is this, little mouse?"

"I'm just trying to figure out who would most benefit from Arthur's demise."

"And have you consulted Merlin about this?"

Her attitude rankled me. "At this point I've nothing conclusive to present to him. When I can show him something informative, I most certainly will inform him."

"Oh, I'm sorry, Allowishes, but that fool Elaine irks me so. I didn't mean to take my frustration out on you." I smiled. I too was a little hasty to judge.

"The girl is trying. I don't believe I've ever encountered a more taxing individual."

~ ~ ~

MERLIN

I was more than a little unsettled. My visit with the King left me feeling hollow. As if I too were becoming a mere husk. With all my training and skills, I was unable to cure him. I could not aid him alone, Morgaine will have to assist me. It is the only course left to us.

Glancing up at the sun, I noted it sat high in the sky. I'd most likely missed the noon meal. Praying Morgaine kept my secret, I hurried to my quarters.

There at the table was the whole troupe. Morgaine caught my eye, signaling she'd not revealed my secret.

"Merlin, I should have waited for you, but they were hungry. My fare is not as magical as yours, but it fills the belly."

I smiled at the lass who was honoring the man she called Grampa. Well, I remembered when she was little, she always came running to me to solve her every problem. Now the shoe was on the other foot. It was I who needed her to fix things for me.

"Morgaine, we must use all our resources, not just yours and mine, but all of us," I said, looking to the table where all, save me and the lass, were seated. Little Allowishes looked up from his writings, cleared his small throat, and reported.

"Great Wizard, I've been plotting out every possible scenario. Taking into consideration, who would have the most to gain, who would have the skill to carry out this heinous deed and lastly who would have access to the king."

I was as proud of the deer mouse as I was of the larger members of the group. His insights are very helpful. Turning to the others, I inquired, "Have any of you anything to report?"

"Fechin and I discovered Guinevere and Lancelot together. They seemed to be very attentive to each other. She wants him to do something and he is reluctant as it is against his duty," the fox relayed.

Fechin then interjected, saying, "I just don't like the look of him. He seems more dandy than knight."

"Are you certain your report is not biased, as you profess not to like the man?"

"Maybe," Flynn said.

"But I have no opinion of the man himself, just what I observed. No man, other than the King or her father, should be alone with the Queen."

"You're quite right. The Queen should be more aware of her station. He actions could endanger Arthur's status as regent for this country. I feared when he wed her she was too immature to be a queen."

"I think not, as you stated before she is foolish, but not devious." I would not condemn the child without evidence.

"She might not be the culprit, but I fear the knight is. All of his actions lead me to believe, he cares not for the King's woman, but his kingdom."

I then heard the click of nails upon wood. I'd not noticed Flynn was missing, but obviously he was returning from somewhere. He was out of breath.

"Whoa, Flynn. What's the hurry?"

Stopping, he gasped, "She's awake, and I think she's leaving. I'll go back and track her, but I wanted you to know."

With that, he turned and ran out.

~ ~ ~

ALLOWISHES

You won't elude me, missy.

When I heard Flynn return, I knew I had to keep track of her. I raced back to Morgaine's quarters and saw her lying on the bed. She's crying. Again. It's a wonder she doesn't dissolve.

She rose from the bed dabbed her eyes with the corner of her apron and started for the door. I had to keep her here until Merlin came.

Quickly I ran across her feet and squeaked as loud as I could. Predictably, she screamed, jumped back onto the bed, and fell to her knees. I stood in front of her just staring. She seemed to regain her composure, so I climbed up the beddings and ran across her feet again. Trying hard not to laugh, as I wished to be frightening, I heard her let out a yowl that would wake the long dead.

Suddenly the room was filled. Everyone gathered around the bed. Flynn chortled, Fechin crowed, Morgaine grinned, and Merlin guffawed.

The girl stood, mortified to be caught stricken by such all-encompassing fear. She started to cry, yet again. The lass has enough moisture to fill a river and quite possibly drown me. I scampered down to the floor and stood in front of the great wizard.

"Well done, Allowishes. I could not have performed better myself." Morgaine moved to Elaine's side and placed her arm about the shoulders of the still sobbing lass.

"Elaine, you must cease your sobs. They serve no end."

"But-But I can't live without him."

"Yes, you can, and you will, happily so. No go wash your face then come back here."

I don't trust her out of my sight. Since she is frightened at the sight of me I will follow her and remain hidden. I assumed she would return to Morgaine's quarters, however she did not. Looking furtively up and down the hall, she quickly raced to the main castle kitchen. I scampered close behind.

She found a jug of water and poured some into a basin. Washing her face and hands she then dried them with the inner side of her apron. Once she appeared sufficiently cleansed, she again surveyed her surroundings, then made a mad dash to the rear door.

The door slammed quickly behind her hindering my pursuit. Though it would take me only moments to find another exit, I now knew no way to determine in which direction she fled.

What will serve better? To attempt to find her on my own or to have Flynn and Fechin assist in my search?

Sometimes endeavors are best performed by one, but this was not one of those times. I hurried back to the main hall to engage my fellows.

~ ~ ~

HAGA

"You fool knight, don't bother me with your petty problems. I gave you what you asked for. What you do with it is entirely your purview, not mine."

"But I am aiding you as well. Does that not count as recompense?"

"It would, were the task completed, but my daughter is not yet upon the throne."

I watched him carefully as he grumbled a response. I told him what I wanted. I'll not settle for less. He knows well the consequence.

"All right, Haga, I'll do as you bid. But the crying child is not to my liking."

"'Twas you who made the plan, not I. Results are all that concern me."

The haughty knight meekly slunk away. Looking this way and that to assure himself, he would not be embarrassed in front of his comrades.

~ ~ ~

ALLOWISHES

My desk was cluttered with research and the books Merlin lent me cover most of his worktable.

I am certain the answer was in the genealogy. It had to be someone who wanted the regency. There is no other scenario that makes any sense.

I was exhausted from constant hours of reading, so tired I did not hear the click of Flynn's nails or the flutter of Fechin's wings. Flynn yipped and caught my attention. I looked down and saw the pair grinning like idiots.

"Well, have you two learned something of great import?"

"Yes," they replied with a single voice. Each of them tried to speak at the same time. Thus, I could understand neither.

"Whoa, slow down, one at a time. Fechin, you first."

The raven flew up onto the table. Her flight disturbed my papers and they scattered in all directions. "Now look what you've done."

Angry, I stomped to the edge of the worktable, grabbed the chain that held Merlin's straightedge, and slid to the floor. Shaking my tiny fist at the fox, I made certain he knew I was mad. Very mad.

~ ~ ~

MERLIN

Allowishes scampered across the rushes, far faster than I'd ever seen the little rodent run. I reached down and scooped him up in my palm. Poor Allowishes he continued to run even as he was upon my hand. Very gently, I cupped my other hand over the poor little deer mouse.

"Allowishes, why do you fret? You know you can easily restore order. Why waste your ire on allies?"

I could feel the mouse push against my hand. Had he come to reason of his own accord? I removed the covering hand and smiled at little Allowishes. The mouse wiggled his large ears and returned the gesture.

"I know, Merlin, I'd just spent so much time searching for an answer. Those two have their heads in the clouds. Thinking of nothing save one another."

"'Tis true, I've noted of late they are quite addlepated." Allowishes nodded and stepped from my palm.

"And what have you concluded from your hours of study?"

"Well," he hesitated, "I've examined each and every possibility. The only thing that appears logical is to search genealogy. Only one who seeks to be king would dare such a foul deed. Furthermore, it must be someone who has substantial proof of legitimacy." My attention was so intent upon the mouse's revelation I failed to realize Flynn and Fechin were still waiting to speak. Flynn barked sharply.

"And, what do you two have to add?" I inquired.

"Merlin, we followed Lancelot all day and night. He spent most of his time in the heraldry room."

Fechin interjected, "Yes, and I saw him take out several pages and secrete them in his tunic." Allowishes jumped up and down.

"Yes, yes, it is as I said. He is altering the heraldry to prove he is a direct descendent."

It is a remarkable deduction and one that has definite merit.

"Fechin, how did he handle the pages he took?" I asked.

"With great care. He rolled them carefully before he put them in his clothing." Flynn started barking and turning in circles.

"And, and he didn't just rip out the pages, he had a special kind of knife. And, and he wore white gloves."

~ ~ ~

LANCELOT

I stood at the edge of the meadow, waiting for Elaine. Damn, I wish she was more comely or less simpering. It would be less difficult to deal with a plain woman of cheerful countenance than a beautiful one who whines constantly. I heard her cry out my name as she raced across the meadow. At least today she seemed in good spirits.

I knew Haga did not want the king dead, but she did not know I frequently switched the potion for the tonic. It would not serve me well if the Queen died before the King. The liquids were not easily distinguished from one another. I would have to be very careful.

"Lancelot," Elaine ventured.

"Have you any news? I've not dared to see Arthur in days. The Queen hovers over him and allows no one to visit. How does he fare?"

"He is improving, Elaine. Slowly, but improving."

"Oh, dear Lancelot, I thank you for all you've done. Getting Haga to mix the potion and tonic was a stroke of genius. I am indebted to you both." It was clear the little chit loved the King, but it shan't take me long to win her affections. She's not the first woman I've seduced, nor will she be the last.

"Yes, my sweet Elaine, you owe me a great deal. Remember that when I next ask you to do me a service. You must comply for our venture to succeed."

"I shall not forget. Dear Lancelot, whatever you ask of me I will do, have no doubt."

"I'm glad you understand, lass." If she is smart enough to do exactly as I say, this will be an easy undertaking. "Now go and seek your love. But have a care, no one must know you are there."

I watched as she grabbed up her skirt and ran to the tower, to see Arthur. I'd seen to it that he had not the potion for a few days, so he would appear much better.

It was now up to me to woo my Queen. She's a young and fickle girl, easily manipulated, who cries for attention. And I shall give her my full attention, once the King is dead. For now, my seduction must be subtle.

Heading for the garden I knew Guinevere favored at this hour, I schooled my features to appear concerned about the King. For the moment Gwen was playing the helpful, concerned wife. She reveled in the attention she received by being the devoted spouse, even though she cared not. Everything was a game to her. How Arthur ever thought she had enough substance to be a queen, I'll never understand. At least Elaine believed her capable of great evil. If she had sympathy for the Queen, it would conflict her feelings. I must continually stress the danger to the king from his wife. Elaine would give her life to save Arthur. However, such heroics are not required. When the time is right, he shall simply pass with no one the wiser as to the cause of his demise. Little perfect wife sat on a bench in the center of the garden the King had specially created for his new wife. Flowers bloomed abundantly and the shrubs and bushes were trimmed to look like various mythical creatures. The sweet, subtle scent of roses permeated the air. She looked up at me with longing in her eyes. She dared not act upon her feelings, as she was still playing the role of dutiful wife. I must act slowly, for if I push the issue, I will lose all I have gained. I've only been at Camelot for a short time. Time enough for the King to treat me as a trusted confidant, but not sufficient time for the Queen to believe I can offer her security, once the king is gone. It is nearing autumn; by Christmas the throne will be mine. Guinevere will fall in my arms in despair over her dead husband. "Ah, my Queen, how do you fare?"

"Lancelot, how good of you to ask. Everyone else only asks of the King's wellbeing. This is a trial for me as well."

"I understand being a caregiver is no easy task. So how are you managing? Are you getting enough rest? Are you eating well? It would not due if you were to fall ill as well."

"Thank you, dear Lancelot. I am well, and greatly appreciate your concern. I am off to dine even as we speak. Would you care to join me?"

"Ah, dear lady, as much joy as that would bring me, I must decline as duty calls. It is up to me to act in Arthur's stead."

"Go then, fair knight, I know Arthur relies upon you."

Chapter 5

· · · · · · · · · · ·

FLYNN

I noted Fechin flying overhead, and indicated she was to follow
the girl, while I dogged the footsteps of Lancelot. She understood
and soon was out of sight.

The knight was leaning against a large rock, examining a piece
of parchment. He'd put on his white gloves before he touched it. He
then carefully rolled it and secreted it in a large pouch at his side.
I'd not noticed the pouch before, perhaps he'd hidden it in a crevice
of the rock? Apparently satisfied with what was on the parchment,
he patted the bag and strode towards the castle.

He did not appear to be in a hurry, but he was very wary. Each
step he took, he stopped to see behind and around him. Holding the
pouch close to his body, he went past the front entrance to the back
of the castle. He quickly drew open the postern door and it closed
behind him. I thought my following him would be thwarted, but a
window ledge that held numerous cooling pies, had an opening large
enough for me to pursue. Those pies smelled so good, I wish I dared
to take one, but my mission was more important than my stomach.

The faithless knight headed for Merlin's quarters. Why I was
not sure, as everyone knows the Merlin does not rise until the sun
is at its highest peak. The man is a heavy sleeper, as he spends long
hours nightly poring over his papers and experiments. It would be
easier to raise the dead than to awaken the mage.

Lancelot took great care to not make a sound. It became clear to me he had no intention of seeking the wisdom of the wizard, he had other plans. He tiptoed into the workroom. Allowishes saw him and quickly hid. Furtively, Lancelot searched the room and when his eyes landed upon the large desk of Merlin, he went directly to it. The Merlin was very orderly and kept all his inks, quills and scraping knives in a large box on the right hand of the desktop.

Lancelot examined each bottle and feather. He was searching for something specific. But what? He then picked up a bottle that appeared to be a clear liquid. When he held it to the light, it had yellow cast. I'd never seen Merlin use this particular bottle. What was in it? Opening the bag at his side he placed the container inside. He stopped, listened, then quit the room. I continued behind him at a safe distance. He did not leave the castle but returned to his own quarters. Knowing I had to stay with him without being seen I pondered how I would accomplish the task.

Fortune smiled upon me. I'd forgotten each knight had a squire who served him and rested in a small room adjacent to his. The lad had to have easy access to his master, thus there was a way for me to enter unseen. It took me only scant moments to enter and find myself a spot to observe the knight.

He was sitting at a small table with the parchment spread out before him. Taking out the strange looking knife I'd seen him use in the heraldry room, he gently took the tool and scraped it lightly against a portion of the parchment. After each pass of the knife he applied the liquid he'd taken from Merlin.

It had a scent somewhat familiar, yet something I remembered without fondness. As he continued to use the strong-smelling substance, I recalled what it reminded me of. It was the same smell as on those yellow things I'd taken from the kitchen. They were bitter and made my mouth pucker. I shook my head at the recollection. Why would he put the juice on a paper of such great value? The damned stuff can eat whitewash, I could only imagine what it would do to parchment.

As there was no way I could understand exactly what he'd done, I would report to Merlin what I observed.

~ ~ ~

FECHIN

I've known Elaine for quite some time, and she was as erratic as the weather. She had more common sense than the Queen but was frequently moody and reasoned with her heart. Her head rarely entered her decisions.

Heading toward the village, she went straightaway to the end of the cottages, crossed the meadow, and went to Haga's dwelling.

The old woman bid her enter, grabbed her elbow, and pulled her into the hut. I'd left myself a listening place the last time I was here and slipped into it soundlessly.

"Haga, you must give me something stronger. He's not getting any better, I fear for his life. It is bad enough he's not in my life, but if he has no life of his own, then I, too, will perish."

"Don't be so melodramatic, you fool child. The potion and tonic I've given you are as potent as possible. Just remember do not mix the two and never give the tonic to Arthur." The old woman sounded annoyed with Elaine. I wonder what her stake in this endeavor is.

"Here, take this new batch," Haga said, pushing a bundle at her and shoving her out the door, slamming it shut behind the girl. I emerged from the thatch to watch her.

She looked all around and appeared lost, unsure of what way she should go. I prayed she got some sense of direction, as I was in no mood to lead her back to the castle. I'd done it before, but it was a tedious process. Ah, there she goes, and on the right track. It is hard to lead someone without them being aware of your assistance.

Once she entered the castle, she went directly to Arthur's quarters. From the hallway, I saw her enter and flew in behind her, unseen. Arthur was completely alone and sleeping. She carefully opened the bundle Haga had given her. Within, I noted two containers exactly alike. Elaine carefully examined both and her features became contorted with what appeared to be abject fear.

"Oh, dear heavens. What am I to do? I don't know which is which," she whispered. She shook herself and then opened each of the bottles. Pouring a small amount into a goblet she sniffed it, then set it aside. Doing the same with the second liquid she selected the first and poured a goodly measure into the goblet. Arthur stirred, and she went to his bedside and gently touched his shoulder.

"Arthur, are you able to take some healing potion?" The King smiled up at her and nodded. Setting the goblet on the table near the bed, she assisted him to a sitting position. He leaned forward and she fluffed his pillows, then gently eased him back onto them.

Arthur sighed. "Did I hurt you?" she asked. He shook his head no. She smiled and put the goblet to his lips, and he drank deeply.

I heard footsteps coming down the hall. Elaine did as well and retreated behind the tapestry. The King watched her hide but said nothing. The footsteps diminished as they passed Arthur's door and continued down the corridor. She emerged from her secret place and tip toed out the door. For some reason that I did not truly understand, I felt compelled to remain with the King. At first, he looked to be in a restful sleep, then beads of sweat appeared on his forehead. He thrashed, turning first one way then the opposite, as if he were having a terrible dream. His face was flushed a deep red. Something was wrong, very wrong.

I rushed to Merlin's workroom. The wizard was not there, only Allowishes, poring over his papers as usual.

"Allowishes," I yelled. He was so intent on his work he did not hear me.

I cawed loudly, and his head jerked up. "What?" he asked.

"There is something wrong with the King. I think he might be sicker."

"Why do you believe he is sicker?"

I explained Arthur's condition and bid the mouse to follow me to the King's quarters.

He was not able to run as fast as I could fly, so I was well ahead of him when he ran into Merlin, who was most likely coming to see his patient.

"Whoa there, Allowishes. Where are you going in such a hurry?" the sorcerer inquired.

"To see the King. Fechin says he is bad sick."

I then joined the pair and informed Merlin about the situation. He grabbed up his robe to his knees and ran the short distance to the King's quarters. He threw open the door and raced to the bedside, where Arthur was still thrashing. His pillows were drenched with sweat and his face had taken on a gray pallor.

"Fechin, find Morgaine and bring her here without delay. Only she will be able to determine exactly what has befallen Arthur. Go!"

~ ~ ~

ALLOWISHES

I'd never seen the mage look so distressed, he was beside himself with fear. His hands shook. Then a great calm came over him and he went to the table with the goblet and sniffed the remaining contents. He then pushed it under my nose.

"Do you recognize the smell? I do not."

"No, I don't know what it is, but I shall do my very best to find out."

Peering into the goblet, I noted the liquid had taken on a purple hue, and the scent grew stronger. The contents appeared to become thicker, as does stale wine, when left in the glass. I took a small twig and stuck it in the substance on the bottom. I held it carefully so it would not be tainted by touching anything else.

I went to my research shelf and withdrew my little book of poisons. There was no time to waste, Arthur is in a dire situation. Page after page, I read, learning nothing. There was not a single notation of anything even similar to the residue in the goblet. Now the scent was fading, but I will remember that stench as long as I live.

The door to the workroom burst open and Morgaine entered.

"Have you found out what it is?" she asked.

"Sadly, no." I hung my head. If we couldn't identify the poison, the King may very well die. Morgaine's features mirrored my own. She, too, knew the situation was most dire.

"I've found nothing, not even something similar," I lamented.

"Fear not, I may have the solution," she said, rushing from the room. "Fechin, go with her and bring the answer to me at once, as soon as she finds it."

~ ~ ~

FECHIN

I followed her to her rooms. It did not take her long to find a large book. That I had to believe had the answer. I'd never seen a book so massive. It must have had at least five thousand pages. She struggled to lift it to her desk. Donning white gloves, she blew on the cover. The dust flew everywhere.

"Do not breathe in the dust," she ordered. I did as I was told. This ominous book reeked of black magic.

"Fechin, you must never speak of this to anyone."

"Not even Merlin?" I told Merlin everything. It is not wise to withhold information from the wizard.

"Especially not Merlin."

"Why not?"

"Just swear never to speak of this book to any living being."

She was agitated, more so than I had ever seen her.

"All right, I swear. I shall not speak of it."

Morgaine said nothing, but with great reverence she opened the huge tome. She ran her gloved fingers reverently over the dark letters. Morgaine was in another world. A world I could neither see nor enter.

From the pages of the book rose a crimson tendril of smoke. Morgaine threw back her head, mouth agape and eyes glazed. This is taking far too long. We've little time to save the King.

Time? Time? Allowishes can turn back time. Why did we not think of this sooner?

Morgaine was lost deep in her own realm and didn't show signs of returning anytime soon.

I rushed from her quarters back to Allowishes. He was still searching for an answer. I cawed, and he looked up.

"Fechin, have you found an antidote?"

"No, but I think I've found a solution. You can reverse time, right?"

"Yes, but only for a short time passed."

"What do you mean?"

"I can go back and hour or two, but more than that my powers diminish."

I was defeated. Thinking I had a solution to the entire mess was both vain and foolhardy.

"Allowishes, what are we to do? Morgaine is in some kind of trance and I cannot speak to her. Whatever she is doing is taking too long!"

The deer mouse looked at me, his eyes near as large as his ears. "I cannot turn back time long gone but, I can halt it for an extended period up to two days."

My feathers ruffled, as if a strong wind blew through the workroom. Maybe not the complete resolution but, more time would be a great boon.

"But you must know," he said.

"I can only halt time for one person."

Only one? But which? To give Arthur more time to heal or Morgaine more hours to find the total rectification. This is a problem far too grave for the two of us.

"Allowishes, stay here and keep searching. I will fly to Merlin and have him make the decision."

"Aye," he replied. I flew out the narrow window and within moments I was at Merlin's side in Arthur's bedroom. It was clear the King was growing weaker. Merlin lifted his head and stared at me.

"Has Morgaine found the antidote?"

"Not yet, but we have found something that should help."

"Out with it you damned black bird."

Merlin never before addressed me as such. He was clearly fraught with terror. Not in all the centuries he'd lived, had he ever encountered a problem he could not solve on his own. This was tearing him apart. The old wizard took several deep breaths to calm himself.

"Well, what is it bird?"

I'm unused to being spoken to in that manner, but in view of his agitated state I'll let it pass.

"Allowishes and I have found a partial solution, but it comes with another problem." Merlin glared, his angst clearly apparent. "And the problem is?"

I explained the situation to the wizard as quickly as I could while he pulled on his long white beard, as he was wont to do when contemplating.

"Fechin, go to Allowishes and tell him to hold Arthur's time, then await my instruction in the workroom with him."

At once I did as I was bid. Allowishes did as well and we settled in to wait. Not an over long period of time passed, when Morgaine appeared. Her clothes were askew, her hair in disarray, and her eyes retained that glazed look, I'd seen before. Merlin arrived only moments later, clearly less disturbed.

Chapter 6

· · · · · · · · · · ·

MERLIN

I knew it. You withheld it from me? The man you call Grampa? Why, Morgaine? Why would you do this? I sighed deeply. As wrong as it was, Morgaine was right. It had to be done.

"I'm so sorry, child, it pains me that you would put yourself in such danger."

"Because, Grampa, I knew this day would come. I also know you would not risk the action and I felt deep within my heart it had to be taken. As I am much younger, the danger was far less for me than you." Morgaine smiled and gently laid her hand on my arm.

"It is done, Grandfather. I've found the answer."

"What would you have us do, Morgaine?" Allowishes asked.

"Fechin, you will search far and wide to find the plant in this drawing."

I reached out and took the parchment. "Morgaine, I know not of this plant. What is it?"

"Alas, I too am unaware of it," she replied, dropping the drawing to the floor.

Flynn walked up to it and placed his paw on it, saying, "I know this plant. It is but a weed. It grows only during the night and blooms very briefly just as dawn breaks."

I was relieved. My dear granddaughter had come through the trial unscathed. Pleased that Flynn recognized the weed and knew of its properties, I bent down on one knee to speak with him.

"Flynn, do you believe the unique qualities of this weed contain the potion that will save the life of the king?"

"Great Sorcerer," Morgaine interjected, "as strange as is the plant, so too is the instruction I've been given for its preparation. We must secure the weed as quickly as possible as the time to make it ready is considerable."

I understood, but in all my travels I've never seen this particular plant. "Flynn," I said.

"As you recognize it, can you procure this strange healing weed?"

"I know where it can be found, but it is some distance from here. It may take too long." Fechin spoke up. "How far as the raven flies?"

"Yes, yes," he replied.

"I can tell you where it is, and you can fly there far faster than I can run."

I was so proud of them. Figuring out the problem's solution without the intervention of magic. These two were a force to be reckoned with. But before I could become comfortable, Morgaine intervened.

"That Fechin can find it quickly is a boon, but according to the directions the elixir must be prepared at the instant the bloom is plucked. And it must be done in a specific manner." Allowishes scampered over to Flynn and looked intently at the scrap of parchment beneath the fox's paw.

"Move your foot, Flynn, so I can read the rest."

~ ~ ~

ALLOWISHES

"All right, I got it, I got it."

Morgaine knelt and picked up the drawing.

"You mean you read the back of the picture and can implement the procedure?" The expression on her face was priceless.

"Yes, my Lady Morgaine, I did, and I can."

Merlin clapped his hands and all eyes turned in his direction. "Now we have a plan."

"Flynn make a map. Allowishes, get what you need for the preparation, and you, you damned black bird," he said affectionately, "You will fly the mouse to the site. Understood?"

I'd never seen the old wizard so masterful. It was as if this were his first lifetime. And I am going to prove to him size does matter. Were I any bigger, Fechin couldn't carry me.

Now this is going to be an adventure. "Is everyone ready?" I called.

Flynn handed me a map. Big that it might be easily read, yet small enough to carry.

Flynn went to Fechin's side and spoke softly to her. "Are you sure you can do this? I don't like it when you are in danger. Life without you has no meaning."

I barely heard her reply, so gently did she speak. "Flynn, you are my heart, I shall do nothing to endanger whatever future we may have."

~ ~ ~

MORDRED (Morgaine's son)

I've been away from Camelot since my mother reconciled with her brother, my father. I wonder will she still champion my cause. Waiting just outside the postern gate, I saw a man I'd not seen before. He appeared to be a seasoned knight. Not by age but experience. He moved as a warrior, cautious and confident.

Usually, other than servants, those who used the rear gate were engaged in some type of nefarious activity. Could this knight be an ally?

I would not risk making his acquaintance without knowing more about him. My dear mother would know exactly who this dandy is. His cocky attitude is apparent in every step he takes. Something is not right here. Camelot has taken on an ominous air. I must determine what is going on here. I moved around to the main gate. No one seemed to give me the smallest of notice.

Neither my father nor the Queen has seen fit to welcome me. Why? Whatever else Arthur is, the man has always been the most gracious of hosts. Looking across the bailey, I spotted my mother, Morgaine, and that old fool wizard she treated better than me. He does not know of my distain, nor will he until I realize my dream. Extending my hand to the old man, I shook his and bowed lightly to Morgaine.

"Hello, nice to see you, my boy," the mage replied.

Mother came forward and enfolded me in her arms.

"You have been so long from Camelot. I've missed you, son."

Feigning interest, I added, "Your faces display despair. Is something amiss with the King? Are we going to battle?" I knew that we would appeal to them.

"Not war, Mordred, but the King is very ill," Merlin answered.

The King is ill? *This could be my chance.*

"What illness has befallen him?" I asked.

Morgaine looked to Merlin, who gave a slight nod.

"We believe he's being poisoned."

"Poisoned?" I said.

"Who would poison a king?"

"My son, if we knew that, perhaps we could save him. We know not who or why," she replied. I decided not to question further, for fear of making myself the prime suspect.

"Mordred, in your travels did you ever hear of anyone who envied Arthur and Camelot?"

"Mother, please, every man envies the King." Many would wish his riches were theirs. But I doubt any would risk killing him.

My mother nodded and tears began to fall. I cannot bear to hear her cry, so I pulled her into my arms to comfort her. It was a feeling entirely foreign to me. She pushed away from me, looked up and within her eyes I saw… love.

~ ~ ~

ALLOWISHES

I never thought I would soar above the trees. What a feeling. Fechin knows such freedom, to be unfettered by gravity.

So, overcome with the majesty of it, I realized I was neglecting my duty.

Ours was a monumental task and should not be taken lightly.

Opening the map, I began to look for the landmarks Flynn notated. Ashamed of my pervious inattention, I was relieved to see Fechin kept us right on track.

The view below was spectacular. Massive gray mountains pierced the sky. Some were tipped with early snow. I pulled gently at one of Fechin's feathers, as I saw the strangely shaped tree that was on the map. Never before had I seen such a deformed tree. The branches curled and twisted back on themselves, the leaves were long and dark sinister fingers reaching to the ground below. The lone tree stood on a high crag in the center of a patch of unusual plants.

Thank God Fechin can fly as there is no other point of access. There was little area to land, so the raven perched on one of the tree's lower branches. Adjusting the pouch on my shoulder I scampered to the ground. I laid out the items needed to prepare the elixir once the flower bloomed. The foliage was so thick I was having trouble identifying the particular plant we sought. As I stared at the confusing patch of vegetation, one plant as if in tandem with the rising sun reached upward to the light. As the petals began to unfold from the center sprang a shower of golden liquid.

"Hurry," Fechin cried.

"You missed it. Try again, but you must catch it correctly as there is only one remaining."

I concentrated and placed my paw near the stem of the last bud. The sun was near to full rising, casting its rays upon the unopened bud. The moment the warmth coaxed the petals open I grasped the stem and plucked the blossom. Placing the flower upside down in the container Morgaine provided, I noted the substance that emerged was a strange greenish gold, it swirled around and around in the glass. Per the instruction, I quickly covered the bottle and placed it in my satchel. I then raced up to the branch Fechin was perched on and urged her to flight.

~ ~ ~

FLYNN

What was taking them so long? The map was very clear, they should encounter no difficulties.

I paced back and forth the entire length of the workroom. It seemed an endless trip. Morgaine and Merlin remained with the King. Thankfully Allowishes halted his time so Arthur would get no worse, while the cure was being sought,

Though it seemed many days had passed, it was in fact only a matter of hours. Then I heard the soft flutter of Fechin's wings. They returned! Entering the large window of the room, I told them to go directly to the King.

Allowishes scampered as fast as his legs would carry him. He was going so fast he slid passed the door to Arthur's quarters. Backtracking, he returned to the King's room and carefully poured the potion into a chalice. Morgaine took the cup and raised it to her brother's lips. It was almost as if a miracle had occurred. The color came back into Arthur's features, and the twinkle returned to his eyes. He once again was the regent of renown. I hoped someday I too would revert to the man I used to be.

I would make it my mission to follow Lancelot until he was caught in his own lies. To use a woman as a dupe is beyond lacking civility; it violated the precepts of knighthood.

I bid the others good day and told them of my plan. All wished me well and warned me of the danger of tracking a knight. I am sure the warning was to a man, but I had the advantage of being an animal. Foxes are the norm in this part of the land, so it was not strange to see one almost anywhere.

~ ~ ~

FLYNN

It was not long before the dopey fool appeared. Fechin went up to the rafters and I stayed hidden behind the large tapestry. The heraldry room was large and well lighted at this time of day. Few people visited there as it was rarely required. Merlin was the only frequent visitor.

The idiot knight was so intent upon his plan he had relaxed his usual vigilance. He started humming and when he went through several cartons, after which he broke into song. I did not know either the tone or the lyrics, something startled him, and he ceased singing.

Talking to himself, he began to exclaim, "This is just what I hoped for. Very little has to be changed." Then he took a book from the carton and checked the spline. Apparently, he found exactly what he sought. Replacing the carton to its proper position, he left the genealogy room, singing to himself.

Fechin flew down to me after Lancelot had left.

"This much is revealing but we need to have witnesses, or perhaps a confession." I nodded as I agreed.

"We have to keep a constant watch on him. Did you see what direction he went in?"

"Yes, he's headed toward the illuminator's shop. It's off the main road just outside of the town. I think we both know why he is going there."

"I dare say we do. But we must be certain. Come on."

We both went outside and followed him as closely as we could, without him noticing us. He was an accomplished thief, as he never looked around or behind him. Most evildoers constantly do their best to assure they are not being followed. His actions led me to believe this was not his first crime. He knew how to move without drawing attention to himself.

We saw him enter the shop and we went around to the back of the establishment, where we could see without being seen.

Lancelot said to the proprietor, "Sir, you do understand that no one other than you and I should have knowledge of this transaction?" The man nodded his assent. Donning white gloves, Lancelot then showed him the pages he'd removed.

"I want these copied exactly save for this single passage." Pointing to an area of the parchment, he then handed the man a smaller piece.

"These words are to be inserted in the place of the removed passage. Also, the design on the shield must be altered. This is the design that must appear."

The shop owner likewise put on gloves and took a closer look at the pieces. "I can do this, but it will take some time. I can have the task completed in no less than eight days."

"If you can do it in less time, I will pay you handsomely. But remember you and only you will know of our arrangement."

The man nodded as Lancelot turned and left. He headed toward the Dancing Duck, a small pub, in the center of the thicket. I wondered at the strange name given the place, but it did not seem to bother any of the patrons. As I looked around the tables and chairs, I thought it might be better named the Drunken Duck. No one in the establishment seem to be sober. Lancelot sat in a chair near the entrance. He pushed the chair back on two legs, leaning against the wall, and proceeded to drink. The tankard of ale he held, the barmaid refilled countless times. He leaned forward until the chair was seated properly, when he saw a large armored soldier come into the pub.

Either the man was a friend, which I doubted, or a mercenary seeking work. The latter proved to be the case. The tall, massive being walked directly toward Lancelot and placed his gauntlets on the table, almost as if a direct altercation were called for. Lancelot smiled and called for more drink for himself and his companion.

I'd never seen the man before. He had the look of a well-seasoned knight. His armor was polished to a gleam and his long dark hair flowed over his shoulders much like a maiden. But there was no mistaking this man for a lass. He pulled out a chair, scraping the legs across the floor making the sound of a scalded cat. All eyes turned to the newcomer, but he did not look away or yield his gaze in any manner.

The stranger was the only sober person in the place. His eyes narrowed as he signaled to the barmaid. She approached and handed him a mug. He took a long pull from the cup and slammed it down on the table. All heads turned at the sound, and a drunken Lancelot lifted his weary head. He was well into his cups.

"Well, what is it that the Great Lancelot cannot handle himself?" the man asked.

"Well, I just thought an expert would be required in this case. You are the fixer, are you not?"

"I am, as you well know. What task have you set before me?" the big man asked. He was larger than any other man I'd even seen. His biceps were as large as tree trunks. The shoulders on him barely made it through the doorway, he had to turn slightly to enter.

Lancelot had a difficulty making the armored being understand him, as he continued to pour down whiskey, and his speech was so slurred he was nearly unconscious.

"I-I want to be King an-and I na-needs you to kill Arthur. No one musst know."

"Well, then," said the fixer, "You better speak a little more clearly and much softer, else you'll never get out of here."

Lancelot looked at him, saying, "Whacha mean? I'n gonna be the king. Nobody ill mess whif me."

The large fellow picked up the knight as if he were a sack of grain. He had to bend his knees to get out of the pub, as with Lancelot on his shoulder the door was far too low to let him pass through. I directed Fechin to leave the establishment and report to Arthur and Merlin.

~ ~ ~

FECHIN

I can't believe a knight of the Round Table would be so foolish. Most knights held themselves to a higher standard. Lancelot's behavior will sadden Arthur, as he considered him a true friend. I do hope Merlin will be kind, but he has never been fond of Lancelot.

I flew as fast as I could to reach Merlin. I did not want to face Arthur alone, as I wasn't sure how to broach the subject. Merlin would know what to do.

He was in his workroom when I found him. He was alone, thankfully, studying a large book. It was one I'd never seen before. It appeared to be very old as the pages crackled when Merlin turned them. I flew and landed beside the massive tome. The old man looked up and nodded to me. Ruffling my feathers and then speaking, I said, "Merlin, Allowishes was correct, Lancelot does wish to be king. And what's more, he told an entire pub of his desire."

"The damned fool. If I'd had but a pence each time that imprudent knight made a ridiculous move, I'd be a very wealthy man. Well, what did he say?"

"That he wants to be king and he wants the big man who joined him, to kill Arthur. He also stated that when he was king no one could gainsay him."

"Who was this big man? Did anyone identify him? Or speak his name?"

"Most of the patrons were drunk and those that weren't fled when he entered. I do remember one of the barmaids called him something I never before."

"And what was that?"

"Earwolff, I'm not sure that's how to say it, but he spelled it to the barmaid."

"Fechin, I know this name, it's Welsh. If he is so named, he must be strong. We can't let him put this plan into motion. Why didn't you continue to follow him?"

"Flynn is tracking his every move, and I will join him when I tell you what I know."

"And is that all of your information?"

"No, the big man had to carry him out as Lancelot was too drunk to walk."

The old man shook his head and went back to studying the large book on his worktable. It appeared Merlin was not impressed with my information. At least he showed no interest. I was more than puzzled by his behavior. Could the mage already have a plan in action? I knew it would be foolhardy to ask, so I just sat next to his book. I must have sat there for an hour. Finally, the wizard rose and left the room. I followed him until I was sure he was going to do something with my message. He went to Arthur's war room, I followed. The King was poring over some new maps he just purchased.

"Merlin, ah, your timing is perfect. Come see this new map. I don't know who made it, but the details are astounding, See, here," he said, pointing to a section that depicted a high tor that also showed the height and pitch. It was very detailed and quite accurate as I'd flown over it many times and it was just as it was drawn.

As I had free rein over the entire castle, I was about to leave when Guinevere entered, but neither Merlin nor Arthur noted her presence. When she saw how engrossed they were with the map, she slipped behind a tapestry. Apparently, she felt excluded from the men's conversation, but felt they would reveal something of interest, if she remained hidden.

She did not have to wait long as Merlin cleared his throat and said, "Arthur, I bear sad news. Lancelot is not what he first appeared to be. I've learned he wants the kingship and your wife as a trophy. He doesn't love her, merely wants her for the title and claim to her lands."

"Merlin, surely you must be mistaken. Gwen is very attentive to me and I've never seen her behave otherwise."

"I wish what I've told you were the only thing that implicates Lancelot. I've been holding this until I could confirm the information. I now am certain, Lancelot has altered pages in the heraldry book."

"To what end?" the King inquired. The look of consternation on this face was almost comical except this was no laughing matter.

I could hear rustling of Gwen's gown as she moved from behind the tapestry. Apparently neither man heard.

"Merlin, tell me exactly what he has done and what the source of your information is," she declared.

~ ~ ~

GWEN

What a fool I've been. Thank God my father has passed and is not here to see my failings. I thought Lancelot was the answer to my prayers. He is the same age as I and owns much land. One would think he would be content with his holdings. But no, he wants to be King.

I didn't realize I'd spoken aloud. Both men turned and stared at me as I emerged from behind the tapestry. As Arthur gazed at me, he turned and covered his face with his hands.

Merlin placed his arm about the King's shoulder to comfort him. "Arthur, she's young and not well informed in the ways of the court. Forgive her this one time. She now knows what a viper he is."

"Oh, I know very well what a fool I am," I said. "And furthermore, I am aware of your kindness that I do not deserve. But, please, both of you know, I will do my utmost to deserve your respect and hopefully once again gain your love Arthur."

"You never lost my love, Gwen, but I am sorely disappointed you were so easily misled. Why do you spy on me? Have you done so often?"

"Nay, Sire, I only done this rashness once, as I wanted to see why Elaine so frequently entered and hid."

"And now you know, have your feelings changed?" the King inquired. "Arthur, I am so filled with shame. Never did I realize I was a simpering coward, but the facts have proven, I am just that."

"I meant your feelings regarding me. My love for you has not changed.

Since you are no longer enamored of Lancelot, are you desirous of me?"

He wants me after all I've done? Either he is a saint, or he really does love me.

"I can't explain it, Your Highness. My impression of Lancelot has altered. You are the king of my heart. And I will do all in my power to prove myself worthy of you."

"Arthur," Merlin interjected, "think carefully she is still a girl and wants to be with a younger man."

She turned and lightly placed her hand on the King's shoulder. "He's right, Sire, but youth and danger no longer hold an enchantment as they once did."

~ ~ ~

MORGAINE

This is a sight I never thought I'd see. Arthur is embracing his wife and they are both crying. I entered the room, saying, "My word, brother, other than your tears, you seem much improved. How did this happen?" Guinevere broke from Arthur's arms and came to face me directly. "Oh, Morgaine, I'm sorry for the way I've treated you. Can you ever forgive me?" Arthur is standing and Gwen asks my forgiveness. Why?

Merlin moved to my side as he did whenever I was confused as a child. "Grampa, please explain all this."

"My dear, I wish a simple explanation would suffice. Gwen has learned Lancelot is not what she believed. He tricked her. And she has also confirmed information he is trying to use her to acquire the crown."

~ ~ ~

FECHIN

I flew down from the rafters to join the others. Merlin is creating a plan to capture Lancelot and prevent him from taking the crown.

The King turned and addressed me. "Fechin, do you know any more than has been revealed here?"

"Not so much new, but I do have positive confirmation of what you have surmised. Lancelot has removed pages from the Book of Heraldry. He then had the pages copied according to his instruction to the illuminator. The man was instructed to insert segments. The illuminator has been arrested many times, but somehow he's escaped actual incarceration."

Arthur fairly exploded with rage. "An illuminator not within a monastery? In my kingdom? Merlin have him brought to me at once!"

The wizard left quickly. The King tried to calm himself by pacing and muttering, while Gwen snuffled, her eyes as large as saucers. "Arthur," she said. "How can I help? Please let me show you my worth."

"Yes, yes, my dear. I've been wrong to treat you as a child. A Queen should know as a King does, all that transpires in the kingdom."

Then the King looked to me. "Fechin, I want you to search until you find Lancelot and when you have, return to Gwen and the two of you follow him."

I nodded and flew out the narrow window. I was just about ready to enter the wood when I saw Lancelot dragging Elaine down the path. She appeared to be his prisoner as he never released his hold on her arm, and she seemed to be struggling to keep at his pace. I followed for moments only when it became clear they were headed for Haga's cottage.

Though not everyone in the kingdom knew Elaine was Haga's daughter, however I did and knew her story as well. Even fewer knew Elaine and Guinevere were twins. Even Guinevere did not know she had a sister.

I went to the roof and burrowed into the thatch. As I had done so before, I quickly found my most comfortable spot.

Flynn was outside searching the barn. He told me the missing pages would likely be hidden there. This was the proof the King needed to prosecute.

I was getting drowsy but was suddenly fully awakened by shouting and screams. Burrowing deeper into the thatch, I could see clearly the confrontation below me.

Lancelot was screaming at the two women. Elaine sounded frightened, but Haga was irate.

"Who do you think you are? You are nothing but a seeker of wealth. No one else matters in your plans. Both Elaine and Guinevere are but pawns in your little chess game."

Then the next thing I heard was a loud thump and the sound of a body dropping to the floor. Guinevere had pushed open the door so hard it bounced off the wall. She struck him soundly with the limb she'd picked up on her way. He lay on the floor.

"Lancelot De Luc, I can hardly believe you only wooed me to obtain the crown and the kingdoms riches."

A soft grumble sounded, followed by feminine-like screeches. Flynn had come through the open door growling menacingly.

Going deeper in the roof covering, I was able to see it was not the women that screamed, it was Lancelot, who was now cowering atop the table, where he had jumped to escape the huge growling, most possibly rabid animal. I thought this was humorous, as apparently did the now laughing ladies.

Flynn circled around the table, still growling. Once the fox was behind him, there was clear path to the door. The terrified knight leapt from the table and ran out the opening. As he ran, he shouted, "This is not the last you'll see of me. I'll be back and you'll be the ones who will be fearful."

~ ~ ~

FLYNN

I should have not allowed him to run. However, the ladies are safe, and I can search for the documents we need. I felt certain they would be found in the barn. At one time I am sure Haga went there frequently, but as she no longer kept animals, there was little need for her to enter.

I searched the main floor but found nothing that should not be in a barn. Knowing how devious Lancelot is, it was more likely he would have secreted the pages in the loft. The way to the loft was by ladder. I am not good on a ladder, but I would have to learn quickly. Very carefully I ascended to the loft. It was dark so I walked slowly to the door that was opened to secure the hay. It hadn't been opened in many years. I pushed against it. It emitted a screech as it swung open.

The bright sunlight was almost glaring. It took a moment for my eyes to adjust. There appeared to be nothing here. However as stupid I thought Lancelot to be, even he would not have hidden a treasure in the middle of the loft. So, I searched along the sloping side walls.

Here was a different matter. Nothing that I could see belonged in a barn. There was a golden suit of armor, a sword, its handle also gold, and a rather large chest. None of these things is usually found in the belongings of a poor old woman. Haga probably hadn't been here in ages. I wonder if she even knows it's here.

I went to the chest and was somewhat surprised to find as it was. It had been padlocked but the lock hung open on the hasp. I poked my snout into the contents. There were many bolts of rich cloth, a silver chalice, and a packet wrapped in a waxed cloth. It seemed strange such riches were unsecured. I took the package and headed out to find Merlin.

~ ~ ~

MORGAINE

Merlin had returned to Arthur's room. The King was sleeping. Though he was much improved, he still tires easily.

"Merlin," I said softly as I had no wish to waken the King. "It appears we have all the facts, do we have enough to submit to the Round Table Council?"

"We'll we have enough to present, but I want to have in my own hand the missing pages."

"Wouldn't the illuminator have them?"

"Perhaps, but considering he is not working legally, he may have destroyed them."

"Well, let us go at once before he thinks more about it, and realizes he is in danger as is his customer."

I don't know if Merlin can move with the speed required. I dare not think what could happen if we can't find the pages. We set out and had not gotten very far when Flynn met us on the way.

"Flynn, what have you there?" the wizard asked.

The fox dropped the package he held in his mouth. I knelt and picked it up. It was wrapped tightly in a waxed cloth, to protect it from the weather, I assumed. Carefully, I opened it and discovered some rolled parchment.

Merlin stopped me from opening it further. "If that is what I think it is, we must get back to the castle before unrolling the parchment," he said, and I was not about to challenge him.

~ ~ ~

LANCELOT

These foolish women will regret disobeying me. They don't realize who they are dealing with. With Arthur gone, I will make this the most revered kingdom in the entire world.

I will be the king this land truly deserves. My man Earwolff will make certain my plans are well carried out. The message I left at the pub will reach him quickly. I'm glad I thought to leave the information before I came to Haga's. I daren't leave the cottage. I must have them in my possession in order to secure my desires.

I waited near the tallest pine next to Haga's place. Elaine usually stayed most of the afternoon. It was starting to rain, and Gwen wouldn't risk damaging her finery. So, I was confident the ladies will tarry with Haga for a while. Earwolff will be here shortly, I know he's fallen on some dire circumstances and will welcome my coin.

The clink of chain mail announced the coming of the soldier.

"Well," he inquired, "For what does the famous and noble Sir Lancelot have need of my services?"

"Nothing that will tax you, my friend. You are to simply kidnap two women," I replied. The burly knight scoffed.

"Where are they? Do I have to travel far?"

"No, they are in the cottage at the edge of the wood. There are no men folk about, so it should be a simple matter for you. You have done this before, I trust?"

"Of course, but if this is so easy why do you not do it? You are a knight after all, supposedly a trusted member of the Round Table."

"I do not wish to be known for this. Thus, you will do it. You are being paid well for your service. That should be all the reason you need."

"Don't be so cocky, little Lancelot. If I felt like it, I could reveal your plans to the King. Remember, I don't like anything about you except your money."

The rain was moving from a deluge to a drizzle, we had to get them quickly before they realize it is stopping.

"Do you have a plan?" I asked.

"Plan? Sure, I'll go in and take them. That's what you want, isn't it?"

~ ~ ~

EARWOLFF

Just who does he think he is? Little popinjay, he isn't worth the sweat off my brow. Had my brother not been such a poor gambler, I would not have to suffer this fool.

I noted the door to the hovel was opening. The sun glinted off the red hair of the woman who peered through the opening. No bigger than a child really, but a woman, nonetheless. This one would give little resistance. She pulled back from the opening and closed the door. Moments later, another lady appeared through the now fully opened door. This one appeared very well dressed and quite haughty. She will, no doubt, react with flying fists and kicking feet. She saw no one so retreated.

This one must be handled quickly. I walked to the door and pounded on it with the pommel of my sword. It made a horrendous sound. Finally, the door was opened by an old hag. Lancelot said two women. Would have been smart for the popinjay to say which two.

The hag asked, "What do you want pounding enough to break the door?"

"I'm looking for two women," I replied.

"Is that the truth or are you coming to rob us?" She tilted her head and spoke through missing teeth. The other two were not dressed as meanly nor were they in need of a washing. Most likely the better dressed and bathed would garner a reward.

I stepped through the door's opening and planted myself directly in front of the bedraggled crone.

"You think you can scare me? Ha!"

She held her hand to her mouth and blew softly into her palm. As I am much taller than she, her sleeping powder did not reach my nose.

"I might not scare you, old woman, but you will do as I bid. Understand?" Still blathering, she sat in the chair I pointed to.

The other two clung to each other as a drowning man holds a scrap of his sinking ship. Even the one who first appeared haughty, was afraid. Their fear was my friend.

"You there in the blue, who are you?"

"I am the Queen and you have no right to detain me in any fashion."

"Detain? Madam, I have no intention of detaining you. I'm just going to take you and your friend. For how long depends on how quickly he pays the ransom." The other one began to snivel.

"Gwen, you're the Queen. Of course, the ransom for you will be paid quickly. What about me? My mother has no funds." Then she started to cry. I cannot stand crying.

"Listen, little one, you two are a set. The two are the same as one. Neither is going without the other." I hope I reassured her, because that was as friendly as I was going to get. I wonder why the pompous ass really wants them?

"Now, ladies, are we going to co-operate or be difficult?"

"If you but speak to the King about whatever your needs are, I am certain he will comply."

"That will not be necessary, Your Highness. The man who hired me will handle such matters." The lady in blue again asserted her haughtiness.

"Good Sir, you are to inform your employer, Lady Elaine and I are to be released at once. Do you understand me, Sir?"

Now this is a joke. How does this woman believe she has any power?

"Lady Guinevere, I shall relay your desire to my employer, but do realize he shall do as he will, without regard for you or your King. That is the truth of it, Your Majesty. Now will you cooperate as I tie your hands and then present you to my employer."

The two women were bound then tied together. I pushed them through the door.

Not twenty feet away stood a man of average size, cloaked in a dark garment. The hood covered his head and most of his face. He did not move, until he saw the crone try to attack me. Raising his arm and pointing at her, by whatever means he possessed, the woman glared then nodded and retreated into her cottage. I directed the women toward the visage on the knoll. Both ladies seemed to grow more frightened, the closer we came to the man with the dark attire.

I did not recognize the person, so I merely nodded and passed by him.

~ ~ ~

LANCELOT

Who does this ignorant giant think he's dealing with? I'm Arthur's most- treasured man. My seat at the Council will always be mine. I will simply move to the King's chair.

Earwolff did not recognize me in my dark cloak. If he's done as I directed, I will no longer have to hide. The ladies will be bound and blindfolded.

I knocked on the door of the hunter's hut and the giant opened it. Peering past Earwolff, I noted the women were unable to see. Lowering my voice so it will not be recognized, I gave Earwolff my instructions regarding Elaine and Guinevere.

"Keep them here, Earwolff, until I return. I've left enough provisions for a week. It should not take longer than that. Arthur will have the ransom note this evening. Treat them well. They are well worth the ransom."

Earwolff will do as he is bid. He's a big man, but in sore need of coin. To look at the man, you would think he was dangerous and mean, however he is a man with a large family. Until he was injured, he easily supported them. A tournament left him unable to fight, so he supported his children working as a man for hire.

It was near twilight so I could be certain Arthur had received word the women were being held for ransom. I went back to my quarters and hid my cloak. Merlin was just coming down the hallway, as I closed my door. I'd never seen him look more dire.

"Merlin, what troubles you? You look as if you received word of war."

The old man shook his head. "Not war, Lancelot, but something just as serious. I must speak with the King," he said as he hurried down the corridor. I hesitated momentarily then turned to follow the mage. It would not do for me to behave as if I did not care about the women. Arthur's war room was only a short distance from my rooms, so Merlin arrived quickly, with me only moments behind.

"Arthur, I just learned the Queen and Lady Elaine have been taken."

"Taken? What do you mean?"

"Kidnapped?" I interjected. "Who would do such a thing?"

The King looked at me strangely, as if he somehow blamed me. I could not risk his discovering he was correct. "Sire, are you certain? I was just in town, having some bridle work done. Could they not also be shopping? You know how they love to shop."

"Did you see them in town?"

"Your Majesty, they are not shopping. This missive states they have been taken and will be returned unharmed, if a ransom is paid quickly."

"Merlin, you do not believe this is true, do you?" The King was already showing fear for the women. His worried face warmed my heart.

"How much do they ask and who are they?" the King inquired.

I dared not speak, for if I appeared to have any knowledge of the matter would arouse suspicion.

~ ~ ~

ALLOWISHES

Sitting at my makeshift desk on Merlin's worktable, I pondered. What made Lancelot so skittish? He always seemed to be hiding something. I dare say I'm not the only one with doubts. But today is the day. I'm not just going to sit here and try to figure out what might happen. I remembered well the feeling of helping, being in the field. It is time I again contributed something to the King besides thoughts and theories. Yes, today is that day. Just because I'm small doesn't mean I can't help.

Just about to leave, when Arthur and Merlin entered. Merlin smiled and nodded. I returned the gesture. Arthur was speaking, not paying any attention to me or even to Merlin.

"We have to rescue those women. Who knows what might happen to them? Where might they have been taken? Does anyone have any answers?"

I was about to speak when the wizard gestured for me to be silent. "Arthur, from what we have learned about Lancelot, I'm quite confident he is the culprit. This man wants to be King, and how matters little to the fool."

"Is there any tavern he frequents? Where does he spend his time? We have to find him and quickly, else he may assume we do not plan to honor his demands." The King took a great breath and sighed. I started to speak but again Merlin silenced me. I quickly wrote on a piece of parchment 'The Dancing Duck.' Merlin nodded and turned to Arthur. "Sire, I've been informed, Lancelot sometimes frequents The Dancing Duck."

Now I knew The Dancing Duck, as I'd followed Fechin there more than once. She said it was a great place to learn what is really happening in the kingdom.

"I've never been in that particular tavern. I thought I knew every establishment in my realm. Not that I frequent taverns, the realm's rule does not afford me the time to visit drinking holes."

I scampered down the table leg holding the scrap of parchment in my teeth and gestured to Merlin that I was going there. He smiled, almost as if he didn't think I could help. Well, he was wrong. I can help and I will.

The Dancing Duck was not far from the castle and I did not have to stick to the road. So, I ran over the meadow and the small copse of trees near the tavern.

There were not too many patrons at this time of day, so I entered the front door that was propped open and moved quickly to the darkened corners. I did not see Lancelot but did note a very large man I'd seen before. He is a known mercenary. I'm not certain, but I believe I once saw him in the company of Lancelot.

The man sat, ordered a drink, and began to brag about his latest task. "I tell ya, it was the easiest kidnapping ya ever saw. Didn't have to go far, just a few feet and the women were scared stiff." He reached out and grabbed a barmaid. "Honey bring me some more and get me enough stew for two. Can't have these ladies die on me. They wouldn't be worth a damn dead."

I didn't have to wait long for the tarnished knight to appear. He strode immediately to the giant.

"Earwolff, I've received confirmation the note has been delivered. The King says he will pay but, he needs two days to amass the monies."

"Sounds good he agrees, but the delay worries me," the big oaf replied. "You don't understand how court works. His request is reasonable."

I smiled to myself. Yes, the King's answer is what Lancelot expected.

This is the best reply for me. It will give me the time I need to put my plan into action. Where the women are being hidden is probably near the castle. Lancelot would not venture far. He is only comfortable with what is in his immediate area of knowledge.

As I made my way back to the castle, I came across Fechin and Flynn.

They said they were sent to confirm what I already knew. "Allowishes," Flynn asked, "do you have a plan?"

"I do, friend fox, and your being here makes it even stronger."

"How?" Fechin inquired.

"We all know Lancelot has some strange fears for a knight. You remember how he fled from Haga's hut when you growled at him? Well, I know he is also afraid of mice."

"Well, we know about Haga's hut, but he won't go back there. Fechin, you fly over the entire realm, have you noticed any other small huts not too far from the castle?"

"There are a couple of hunters huts not far from the Southern side. One is in bad condition, not even a roof. But the other is at least habitable. It's small but it has a roof and a door."

I nodded. This revelation was even more helpful than the first. This enhances my plan further. There were few places with windows on the southern side. There were no guards on this entrance unless we were at war. Arthur had kept the peace for many years. However, if he didn't get well and we fail to thwart Lancelot, war is almost certain.

Fechin was listening closely and finally spoke.

"If we believe Lancelot can cause the demise of Camelot, we must inform Merlin at once."

Dang, there goes my chance to be a hero. I wanted this plan to make me more than a studious mouse. But if the country is truly in jeopardy, I must do my part even if it is only a small piece.

Flynn was pacing back and forth, back and forth. Finally, he stood stark still and growled deep in his throat.

"Fechin is right. We must notify Merlin, but not until we free the ladies."

"But what if something goes wrong? We would be the cause of Camelot's failure," I squeaked. Now I was not thinking of only myself. There was too much at stake for three animals.

"Hey, Allowishes, have a little faith. I know you want to be the savior and you deserve to be. Trust me we can do this. And we will need the help of a human, just not Merlin."

"Who then?" I was growing more trepidatious by the moment.

"You remember the stable boy who tends Lancelot's horse? He's not fond of the knight either. He's a good lad, but always makes it just a little bit difficult for his sire. He'll be glad to help put him in his place."

Fechin spoke excitedly. "Flynn is right. Todd is a modest man and one who will be well pleased to see Lancelot gets his due."

I forced the lump in my throat to move to its proper place. The stable boy would be a big help. I hadn't figured how to unbind the ladies. This Todd could do it with ease since he had hands and most likely a knife. But we had to scare Lancelot from his wits. That I had planned carefully.

"You're right but we still need to frighten the knight beyond his reason. Where fear chases out logic."

"Well, what is your plan and how do we help?" Flynn asked.

I cleared my throat and proceeded to impart my plan. "We know fear is the only way to capture him. But we must watch for the moment he is alone with the Queen and Elaine. We'd be the foolish ones if we try to capture the giant."

Fechin spoke up. "And we cannot risk the lad being hurt. Never mind what we can't do. What can we do?"

"First we gather as many of our own kind as we can. I will be able to get many mice to assist. Next Fechin will get enough ravens to darken the skies. And then Flynn will bring in the foxes. I think perhaps it would be wise if the foxes could appear to be rabid. Is this possible Flynn?"

A wide grin crossed the features of the fox. "Not only is it possible but I know exactly how to do it."

Fechin cocked her head. "What do you mean you know exactly how?"

Flynn explained, "I was orphaned as a very young kit and had no one to show me how or what to eat, so if it smelled good, I ate it. I came across a white berry that had a pleasing aroma."

Fechin ruffled her feathers. The raven was annoyed. "Flynn get to the point. How is this berry going to help us?"

"Well, when you bite into this berry you get white stuff all over your mouth, even on your snout. It's foamy and it sticks to your fur."

"Ah, yes," I replied, "I know this plant they are all over the kingdom. He's right. It does make a creature look like it's rabid."

Chapter 7

· · · · · · · · · · ·

LANCELOT

I waited just outside of the hunter's hut for the big man to appear. There could be no time lapse between his watch and my own. Elaine was a little more cunning than the Queen, and if not constantly watched would escape. The big man emerged from the hut, and I stepped up immediately.

"They're fine. They have just eaten and again are sleeping."

"Very good, Earwolff, I'll take over here and you go to The Dancing Duck," I directed the man.

Enough time had passed that Arthur would have secured the monies. Soon, very soon, it would all be mine. And it won't take long until I can once again capture Gwen's heart. What worth is there to a kingdom without a beautiful queen? Elaine was softly snoring, but Gwen awakened.

"Who's there?"

To answer in my own voice would be foolhardy, so I spoke in a tremulous tone. That of a weak old man.

"Fear not, my child, no harm shall come to you."

"Are you a priest?" she asked.

"No, lass, just a wanderer. I'm aiding an old friend, by making certain you are well cared for."

"Well cared for. Sir, that is a cruel statement. Were I well cared for I would not be here in this filthy place. I can feel the grit seeping into my slippers. This is not a place for a Queen. Release us at once!"

When she is angry the Queen is formidable. Once I tame her, she will truly be the Queen I require. Now Elaine is awakening.

"Gwen, is there someone here?"

"Yes," Gwen replied, "But I fear he will not aid us."

"Why is he one of our captors?"

"I don't think so. He sounds old."

Elaine was unusually quiet, but I could see she was planning something. She was quite cunning for a woman. I quickly drew my hood up and around my head in case whatever she was planning allowed her to recognize me.

Elaine threw herself to the side, tossing both her body and the chair she was tied to onto the dirt floor of the hut. I scurried back further into the shadows.

Gwen cried out, "Elaine, are you all right? What was that noise?"

"I knocked the chair over. We're getting out of here."

"How?" Gwen screamed.

"We're prisoners, captives. We're tied up. We can't escape."

It was almost as if Elaine could see me. She moved to the rack where hunters placed their pelts and scraped her head against it. As she rubbed her face against the rack the blindfold caught on a splinter and was pulled from her eyes. Before she could turn and see me, I slipped out the door.

At once, I was attacked by hordes of mice. God, how I hate rodents. The crawled on my feet, then up my robe squeaking and biting my flesh. I screamed with every fiber of my body, hoping to free myself from this foulness. I could barely breathe as the gray furry creatures crawled over my head.

And from somewhere came a guttural growl, more fierce than I'd ever heard before. From the mouth of these orange curs, white foam dripped. They were rabid. I would die!

I started to run, but to no avail. Following me were hundreds of screeching ravens. Diving at my head and pecking my face. Now they try to blind me, as the women also lacked sight. I shaded my eyes and ran faster than I ever believed I could.

They were all chasing me. I could hear squeaking, growling, and the flapping of wings. Faster and faster, I ran, my hands covering my eyes.

Suddenly I stopped.

~ ~ ~

ARTHUR

We received the ransom notice delivered by a messenger I'd never before encountered. The lad was polite, but frightened. It wasn't difficult to determine the cause of his fear, as most of the men who frequented The Dancing Duck were not the friendly type. The note was written in a hand I did not recognize. Merlin and I determined it would not be wise to take many men with us, so the two of us and a small guard set out to find the kidnappers. We knew Lancelot frequented the tavern, so our search started there. Merlin entered and sat alone in a dark corner, listening. I remained outside, so I could spot anyone coming or leaving. I did not have long to wait. A large man emerged, dressed in full armor. Though I'd never seen him before he behaved in a suspicious manner. I watched carefully to see in what direction he traveled. Very shortly Merlin came out. He smiled and asked, "Have you ever before seen the fellow who just came out?"

"I don't think so, but he is acting strangely. I intend on following him."

"My thoughts exactly," the old wizard replied.

We were on the road only a short time when I spotted a man running with his hands over his eyes and hundreds of ravens were diving at him and pecking his head. Chasing him were a multitude of mice, followed by a vast amount of foxes. I don't think I ever beheld a stranger sight. The man was running as fast as possible and ran headfirst into a large oak.

"Merlin, look. I don't think I've ever seen anything more moronic." The old man shielded his eyes and squinted.

"Arthur, is that Lancelot at the base of that tree?"

"Yes," the King answered.

"That is the poor fool. What's more, he is out cold."

The area seemed flooded with mice, foxes, and ravens. I recognized Allowishes. His little chest is puffed out so big you'd think he was a bullfrog. Most of the creatures were dispersing, only Allowishes, Fechin, and Flynn remained. Merlin knelt to be at eye level or as close as he could come, to speak to the mouse.

"Allowishes, my boy, you've done it!" the old wizard said, as he scratched the head of the deer mouse.

"I'm well pleased with you and your plan, little mouse. The execution of this is worthy of a military general."

"Thank you, master wizard. Now let's tie him up so he cannot escape. And we must also secure the large fellow." Allowishes could accept the compliment, but not overdone praise.

The mage clapped his hands and exclaimed, "On that issue there is no problem, as I placed a magic barrier around him as he left the tavern. He cannot escape as he is held in my power, and one cannot aid him as he cannot be seen by any, other than us."

"I am well pleased with you and your plan, little mouse. The execution of this is prime magic." I could only nod and smile. These small creatures had accomplished what no man can do. Amazing, simply amazing.

"Arthur, these men must be rewarded, but how? Foxes, ravens, and mice have no need for coin."

"I agree, Merlin. But you have within your power to grant each their greatest wish."

"How can I know what that might be?"

"For an old, well-experienced wise mage, you sometimes are a dolt. They speak. Ask them."

"The matter of the intrepid trio is easily settled, but the problem of Lancelot remains," the sorcerer replied.

"He must be punished, I know, but I trusted him. This is something I wish I never had to deal with."

The man was my most valued knight. I could depend on him in every situation. But he betrayed me in the most vile fashion. I love my wife and she has repented. Her, I can forgive, but Lancelot is another matter. To plot and plan against me is unforgivable.

"He must be held to account. What shall I do, Merlin?" The old man sighed and placed an arm about my shoulders.

"Take his spurs and banish him."

~ ~ ~

ALLOWISHES

This is even better than I imagined. It's like a huge party. Everyone is here, even folks I don't know. I wish my folks were still with us. Mother would be so proud. And me Da wouldn't think I wasted my time studying. He told me, often enough, I was frittering away my life with my nose in a book.

I was happy. Sadly, my two friends were not. We were all riding on the huge horse of Lancelot's. The animal had a large flat back. It was like riding a big boat on a calm sea. But why were they sad?

It was a long way to the castle and the street was crowded with well-wishers. It seemed we had bested the worst man in the realm. Lancelot was once well regarded, someone to look up to. Now he was someone to be spat upon.

Each step we took drew us closer the vast courtyard. I'd never seen a castle so large.

"Flynn, we caught the bad guy. He's no longer a knight and he's gone. He'll never cause anyone in Camelot harm. Why do you and Fechin look so sad?"

"Allowishes, this is your dream. Everything you hoped for. Right?"

His question puzzled me. Everything was great for everybody. Why isn't he happy? And why is she so morose?

"Yes, this is just what I've always wanted. Why aren't you two elated? We've saved Camelot and reunited our King and Queen. Isn't that all good?" Flynn looked at me with the saddest eyes I've ever seen. "Fechin and I have been working close with one another."

"So?" I replied.

"We fell in love, little mouse."

"I don't understand."

"We are sad because Fechin is a bird and I'm a fox. We can never mate, we can't have children, and we can't build a life together."

Merlin must have heard our conversations. We all stood in a line in front of the huge structure. Merlin walked back and forth in front of us, his hands clasped behind his back.

"My friends, I've been reminded I can give each of you your fondest wish. I know you have no need for coin. So, tell me what has the most meaning for you?" I spoke up at once. "You mean I can have anything I want?"

"Yes, Allowishes, you can go anywhere, be anyone, at any time. What is your greatest wish?" Now I was confused.

"You said I can have anything I want."

"Yes, you can. What is it you want?" The old mage smirked. This is more like it.

"I want my own workroom, with a real my-sized desk. And-and a door with my name on it."

"You shall have it," Merlin stated.

"In the corner by the window is your workroom." I was so happy I could barely contain myself. But what of Flynn and Fechin?

"Merlin, I am delighted with my gift, but I had help. What will you do for them?"

"Well, my friend, that is up to them. They will of course be rewarded." The old sorcerer turned to the pair who had not yet expressed their wishes.

"Understand, though you are both alone I cannot conjure a family." Flynn stood very close to Fechin.

"Great Merlin, we do understand that. But can you give us the power to create our own family?" The old man was taken aback.

"Well, I suppose so, but remember one of you must change in order to mate. Fechin, are you willing to be a fox? Or, Flynn, would you rather be a raven?"

The pair looked at each other. Their expressions were of fear and terror.

"No, no, no," they cried out. "We want to be like you. Human."

"Whew, that can be done at once. Don't have to figure in gestation periods. Now, are you sure you want to be like me? I will live a very long time, a great expanse of time. The friends I make will pass long before me. Or would you prefer to be like most humans such as Arthur and Guinevere?"

"Yes, yes, yes. That is what we want. To be human, to be man and wife. To marry and start a family. Is that too much to ask?"

"Of course not." Merlin smiled.

"For all you two have done, it is actually a simple request."

Epilogue

. . . .

ALLOWISHES

The air is filled with excitement. This spectacular is even greater than the King's wedding. Guinevere had an amazingly beautiful dress, but in my humble opinion, the garment Fechin is wearing far exceeds what I know of beauty. Her hair is as dark and shiny as her own wing was. The dress only showcases her loveliness.

Flynn is all fancy in a suit with a cape, and even Merlin is dressed up. The little priest from the castle chapel was waddling up the hill that leads to the much-decorated hall. Though they had little time to prepare for this wedding, the ladies of the castle had outdone themselves. There were garlands strung from one end of the room to the other. The rushes are perfumed with the most pleasant herbs and flowers.

A small group of men were tuning up their instruments and then the room became hushed. Everyone turned to look at the beautiful bride and she slowly walked to meet her mate. Her groom seemed to have forgotten how to breathe and his eyes widened to see the magical sight before him.

I sat upon Flynn's shoulder, as he had chosen me to be the best man. Fechin approached on Merlin's arm then stepped beside us. I held the small box from the silversmith that held their wedding rings.

The ceremony was swift and silent, only the pair responding to the priest's questions. As they proceeded back down the long aisle, the crowd broke into shouts of congratulations.

~ ~ ~

Gentle readers, I hope you have enjoyed the tale of Flynn and Fechin. Remember your desires are not always the same as those with whom you share an experience. We each have our own path to travel. To keep current with the newest fox tales, check out my website www.deecareybooks.com.

Also from **Dee Carey**:

FOX TALES

Two Tales of Love Mark of the Fox

Can an enchanted fox and a scarred prince follow the predestined course the Druids have set for them? They fight against the constraints of royalty, but in the end the falconer becomes a willing regent and the fox, his more- than-willing wife.

The Fox and the Swan

To save her family, a girl becomes a swan. The man she loves is enchanted by a witch into a fox. Can the pair unite as humans and save her family? True love triumphs over evil with the aid of a druid, a bishop, and a goddess.

Available now on Amazon: **FOX TALES**

THE CRIMSON VIXEN

The preordained couple meet when Leigh discovers an orphaned fox and keeps her as a secret companion. In time it is revealed his Kit is also a fierce female pirate. The Druids determine the pair are destined to rule Ireland. As a fox she is clever. As a woman she is enchanting. Can Leigh set aside his devotion to King Arthur to be with the woman of his dreams?

Available now on Amazon: **THE CRIMSON VIXEN**

FOX TALES II

Two tales will enchant and bring to you the joy of magic, faith, courage, and the most powerful force in the universe: Love

Can Sean save himself and his friends from the grasp of the most foul? Can Merlot and LaRoux follow their preordained paths to save church and country?

Available now on Amazon: **FOX TALES**

THE FOX AND THE MERMAID

Can a woman, who is actually a seal, and a fox, who might be a man, overcome a man who is an ancient Questing Beast?

Only when those afflicted can realize they must cooperate in order to overcome evil do they prevail.

This story focus is upon loyalty, teamwork, and trust.

Available now on Amazon: **THE FOX AND THE MERMAID**